FOCUS ON THE FAMILY®

The *Nikki* Sheridan Series

Tangled Web

by Shirley Brinkerhoff

D0452218

BETHANY HOUSE PUBLISHERS

MINNEAPOLIS, MINNESOTA 55438

Tangled Web
Copyright © 2000
Shirley Brinkerhoff

Cover illustration by Cheri Bladholm

A Focus on the Family book.
Published by Bethany House Publishers
A Ministry of Bethany Fellowship International
11400 Hampshire Avenue South
Minneapolis, Minnesota 55438
www.bethanyhouse.com

Printed in the United States of America by
Bethany Press International, Minneapolis, Minnesota 55438

Library of Congress Cataloging-in-Publication Data

Brinkerhoff, Shirley.
    Tangled web / by Shirley Brinkerhoff.
        p.   cm. — (The Nikki Sheridan series ; 5)
    Summary: Nikki's eighteenth birthday is the beginning of a series of problems which test her growing faith, including her parents' possible divorce, fear of losing the young man she loves, and a dangerous meeting with someone she meets on the Internet.
    ISBN 1-56179-737-5
    [1. Christian life—Fiction. 2. Mothers and daughters—Fiction. 3. Divorce—Fiction.] I. Title.
PZ7.B780115 Tan   2000   99-053733
[Fic]—dc21   CIP

00 01 02 03 04 05 06 07 / 15 14 13 12 11 10 9 8 7 6 5 4 3 2 1

To Jeanne,
sister and friend

❧ *One* ❧

NIKKI KNEW SOMETHING WAS WRONG, just by the way her mother was driving.

Instead of guiding the shiny, green Saab into the driveway in her usual let's-have-no-nonsense-here style, Rachel Sheridan turned the car slowly, the tires crunching hesitantly over the gravel. Instead of shutting the door sharply and striding confidently up the sidewalk, Rachel sat for an extra few seconds in the front seat—then pushed the door open gradually and looked around the yard, almost as though she was confused at finding herself here.

Mom, what are you doing? Nikki thought, watching from behind the screen door of her grandparents' house.

Nikki pushed open the door and was knocked off-balance by Gallie, her grandparents' golden retriever, who squeezed past her to get outside. The dog galloped down the front porch steps, barking with his usual exuberance, and skidded to a stop within inches of Rachel Sheridan's immaculate beige-linen heels.

Gallie wagged his entire body in anticipation. Rachel, however, seemed oblivious to the 85 pounds of shining, golden canine waiting for her attention.

Nikki followed in Gallie's wake, but slowly. "Hi, Mother. Did you have a good trip?"

There was no response. Rachel seemed to take forever unfolding herself from the car, then stood next to it. Still she said nothing.

Nikki tried again. "Where's Dad?"

Rachel frowned. She seemed disturbed, almost puzzled, by the question. "What do you mean, Nicole?"

Turning both palms up, Nikki spoke slowly and distinctly as if to a toddler. "I said, *where's Dad?* When you called and said you were coming, I assumed that both of you were—"

"I said *I*, Nicole. *I* was coming, that's all."

Rachel took a deep breath and stood up straight, as if willing herself to get with the program. Reaching inside the car, she popped the trunk, then brushed past the still-hopeful Gallie on her way to the back of the car.

She reached inside the trunk and pulled out a small, beige leather overnight case, then shut the top quickly, but not before Nikki saw two things: that Rachel's flawlessly-manicured fingers shook as they closed around the case handle, and that the trunk was filled with other beige leather suitcases, at least three more.

"So what's with all the luggage? Don't tell me—you're running away from home, right?" Nikki asked, trying to make her voice light.

Rachel straightened her shoulders and turned toward the house, overnight case in hand, as though she'd made some kind of decision. "What do you say we put off the question and answer session till later, Nicole? Your grandparents have their hearts set on giving you a wonderful birthday party, and I don't want anything to— well, to spoil it."

"But why would anything spoil—"

"*Please*, Nicole," her mother said, in a voice that was not a request. "And don't mention the extra luggage to your grandparents, either. I'll tell them myself, later on. For now we'll say . . . we'll just say . . . that your father had something come up at the last minute with his latest trial."

What is going on here? Nikki thought in panic. She opened her mouth for one more try at forcing her mother to talk, then closed it again. There was no use arguing with Rachel. There never had been, not in all of Nikki's 18 years. She fell into step behind her mother, eyes fixed on Rachel's slim back, clad in a beige silk suit that moved fluidly with each graceful step.

Nikki swallowed hard and relaxed her face so that she looked— at least she *hoped* she looked—calm and carefree for the party. But inside her head, thoughts were whirling at lightning speed, probing every detail of the phone call from her mother that morning.

I should have paid more attention, she thought guiltily. *I knew something was going on by the way Mother was talking, but all I could think about was Jeff.* There had to be some clue in what Rachel had said, something in that phone call that would help Nikki figure out what was going on. She went back over every word.

She'd had no idea what was coming when she answered the phone and heard her mother's voice that morning. Nikki'd been too busy getting ready to meet Jeff Allen to pay close attention to whatever Rachel Sheridan was saying.

At the thought of seeing Jeff again—now that she could finally admit to herself how important he was to her—Nikki had gladly blown a major hole in her carefully-hoarded stash of money for school clothes. The white denim shorts and new sleeveless linen top she hoped he would like had cost far more than she would normally have spent. So had the new make-up and the highlights in her shoulder-length, curly dark hair. But somehow, it all seemed worth it, if she could get Jeff to care about her the way he used to.

So with her mind almost totally on Jeff, she'd maneuvered the cordless phone into position between her left shoulder and ear, leaving both hands free to tie her sneakers so the phone call from her mother wouldn't slow her down.

Rachel's voice was strangely hesitant. "I thought—perhaps—I'd come up to Michigan tonight," she began. "For your birthday party."

Nikki's fingers stopped tying, mid-bow. She straightened up, then grabbed at the phone as it slipped off her shoulder. "You're coming all the way up here? From Ohio? For my birthday?" The string of questions sounded inane, even to her.

Rachel's laugh was strained. "You make it sound like we're four days apart, Nicole, instead of four hours."

Try four light-years, Nikki thought. But that wasn't the kind of thing you could say out loud—not to your own mother, anyway. "But what about that reception thing you and Dad had to be at? For the politician or judge or whatever? I thought you said it was some big deal you couldn't miss."

There was an awkward pause. "Plans have changed. Anyway, I'd prefer to be at your party, Nicole," Rachel answered finally. "Turning 18 is—well, it's an important birthday. And after all that's happened this year, I would like to spend some time with you. To work on things, on our relationship." Rachel sounded as though she were picking her way through land mines.

Bending over, Nikki yanked out the half-tied bow in her shoelace. *You can't work on something that was never there in the first place.*

Her slender fingers set the white laces into loops, then stretched and knotted jerkily. On the last tug, a lace snapped off in her hands. Looking at the ragged end dangling from her fingers, she sighed loudly into the phone.

"Well, I guess that says it all," her mother murmured in response.

"No! Wait a minute!" Nikki rushed headlong into an explanation. "You don't understand. I was tying my shoe and the lace broke off in my hand. And I was supposed to meet Jeff to go jogging 10 minutes ago and we probably don't have another lace around here. *That's* why I sighed, okay? You just caught me off guard."

Like always, Nikki thought. Stepping to her grandparents' kitchen junk drawer, she pushed aside the wooden clothespins and yellow plastic corn-on-the-cob holders and outdated coupons from Taco Bell. *Maybe there's a shoelace in here somewhere.*

"I'm glad to know that's all it was," Rachel said. "Because there are some things we need to—well, let's just say we need to talk."

Nikki stopped rummaging through the drawer. The strangeness of her mother's tone was beginning to register. "Talk about what, Mother? Would you mind being a little clearer? Is something wrong?"

Rachel gave a short laugh that did nothing to set Nikki's mind at rest. "I don't think this is the kind of situation we can discuss over the phone, Nicole. Some things are just too . . . difficult . . . to talk about this way."

Uneasiness began to gnaw at Nikki's stomach. She closed her eyes and tried to ignore it. *This is supposed to be my special time with Jeff. Besides, she's probably being overly dramatic, making a big deal out of nothing.*

The screened porch door slammed, signaling Jeff's arrival. "Let me guess," he called, his voice loud enough to be heard inside the kitchen. "I've been stood up again, right?"

Nikki shifted the phone to her other ear, pawing through the odds and ends in the drawer one last time. "I'll be there in a minute," she said.

"Excuse me?" Rachel's voice was back to its usual clipped, precise cadence.

"Sorry. Just talking to Jeff."

Jeff's tall frame filled the kitchen doorway then, and he rolled his eyes in mock despair when he saw her. "Oh, no! It's *worse* than being stood up. She's on the phone!"

Nikki made her voice sound resolute. "Look, Mother. I'm sorry, but I really need to go. Jeff's waiting. Since you don't want to talk till you get here anyway, could we hold off till then?"

Rachel paused—just a heartbeat longer than normal, Nikki thought. "Yes. That's probably best. I'll see you tonight, then."

For a moment Nikki thought she heard her mother's voice break on the word "then." After the *click*, she wasn't sure.

She stared at the phone in her hand for a few seconds, uncertain. Finally she shook her head. *This is my time, mine and Jeff's. She's making a mountain out of a molehill, like Gram always says.*

～

Now, though, crossing the boards of the front porch to her birthday party, Nikki could see she'd been wrong. Something really was going on—something big—but there was no way to make Rachel talk until she was good and ready. *I ought to know that by now,* she told herself, following her mother through the front doorway.

Watching the smiles and hugs between her grandparents and her mother, knowing all the while that Rachel would do something after the party to burst this bubble, Nikki felt herself shudder. It was like being forced to lie, watching and knowing and not being able to say anything.

It's just like Mother to ruin even my birthday party, Nikki thought, then caught herself and resolutely tried to turn off the bitterness. After all that had happened this past year, and all she had worked through regarding her parents, she was determined not to slide back into the anger that had trapped her for so long.

It helped that Marta, Rachel's younger sister by 10 years, turned her white Taurus into the driveway behind Rachel's Saab at that point. Nikki ran back outside to meet her, and for just a few minutes, put aside her worries over Rachel.

"Aunt Marta!" she cried. Marta hugged her hard, as though they hadn't seen each other just a few days before. "Thanks for coming all the way back here for my party!"

"You don't think I'd miss your birthday, do you, Nik? Although—" she added, reaching with both hands to smooth the gray-streaked blond hair their hug had dislodged, "—I must say it's a little inconsiderate of you to get this old this fast. You're making me feel absolutely ancient."

"Oh, stop!" Nikki said, laughing. "Nobody could think you were old."

It was hard to think of Marta as anything other than a friend. She'd been there for Nikki during Nikki's pregnancy and the birth of her baby the winter before. Since then, Marta, who traveled frequently in her job as a musicologist, had gone to great lengths to spend extra time with her niece. She'd found a way to take Nikki along on two work trips in the past six months—the first to California, the second to Virginia—which had strengthened their relationship even more.

Marta stretched into the car to grab her suitcase, but Nikki stopped her. "Here—let me get that."

Marta looked at her, surprised. "Why? I'm perfectly capable of doing it myself."

"Yeah, well, really old people shouldn't carry heavy stuff like this."

Marta swatted at her playfully as Nikki turned toward the house with the suitcase. "You don't deserve to hear this, wretched person that you are, but you look especially pretty in that outfit. Have I seen it before?"

Nikki smiled down at her burgundy jumpsuit that was covered with tiny straw-colored leaves. "I had it last summer, before I came up here. Of course, I couldn't wear it when I was pregnant, and you know how long it took me to get the baby weight off so I could fit back into my stuff."

"Well, you look great, Favorite Niece."

"*Only* niece."

"Right." Marta grinned at the old joke before she went on. "Have you heard anything else from Carly?"

Nikki's smile turned wistful as she thought of Jeff's younger sister. Carly had gone with Aunt Marta and Nikki on the trip to Virginia—only to be diagnosed with an eating disorder while they were there.

"I got a letter from her today, actually, but it didn't say much. She's just getting used to things at the clinic. I think she'll do really well there, though, and so do her parents and Jeff, 'cause she's absolutely determined to beat this thing."

Nearing the porch, Nikki stopped. She set her aunt's suitcase on the sidewalk. "Aunt Marta? Can I ask you something before we go inside?"

Marta turned toward her and nodded.

"Do you know—I mean, do you have any idea—what's going on with my mother? Something's bothering her. She brought all this—" Nikki broke off, remembering her mother's request. "I just wondered if maybe you knew if something was wrong," she finished lamely.

Marta looked at her steadily. "I'm afraid I'm in the dark on this one. Do you want to tell me what's worrying you?"

Nikki frowned. *I'd love to tell you*, she thought. *But I can't.*

There was a burst of laughter from inside the house. Nikki's grandmother called outside to where they stood. "Nikki? Nikki, we can't very well start your party without you!"

Nikki glanced back at her aunt and gave a half shrug. "Maybe later, okay? We probably ought to get inside."

Two

THE HOUSE BEGAN TO FEEL FULL once Dr. and Marlene Allen arrived, followed by Jeff and his younger twin sister and brother, Abby and Adam. Arleta, Gram's best friend, bustled in with a huge, glass bowl of fruit salad in her hands and made straight for Nikki, unaware, as usual, of the volume of her voice.

"NIKKI, NIKKI, I *HAVE* TO TALK TO YOU ABOUT—"

She broke off as Keesha Riley strode in behind her, dressed in an orange sundress so bright and so short that even Arleta appeared to forget everything she'd been about to say, unable to take her eyes off it. Five-inch gold hoops in Keesha's ears and long, gold-painted fingernails also seemed to fascinate the older woman, but it was Keesha's hair that surprised everyone the most.

"You got rid of all your braids, Keesha!" Nikki stared in amazement at her coarse black hair, which now measured barely an inch in length. "*When?*"

Keesha grinned and put one hand behind her head like a model. "A couple weeks ago. Right after you left with your aunt, I guess. I got tired of prying Serena's fingers off the beads, you know? Besides, this saves me a heap of time."

Gram stepped in to take the fruit salad from Arleta's hands. Gently Gram prodded Arleta toward the dining room, murmuring, "Whatever you were going to tell Nikki, it can wait a few more min-

9

utes, Arleta. We're ready to start." With Nikki's grandparents, mother, and aunt there, too, the house seemed filled to overflowing.

For Nikki, the highlight of the party was one small detail that probably only she and Grandpa noticed—Gram's quiet smile of pride as she set the birthday cake that she had baked herself, 18 candles flickering brightly, in front of her granddaughter. Baking, frosting, and even carrying the cake by herself marked her triumph over a year of sudden, shocking disability from her stroke the summer before. This cake had none of Gram's usual fancy piped rosettes or lettering, true—things that required fine motor control were still beyond her—but it was a far cry from lying comatose in a hospital bed, as she had been last year.

Nikki caught her grandpa's gaze over the candles and winked, then reached up to hug her grandmother tightly. "It's a *beautiful* cake. Thank you," she whispered against Gram's gray hair.

"Next year I'll do better," Gram whispered back, then spoke loudly enough for everyone to hear. "Make a wish and blow, Nikki. Quick, now, before wax drips all over the frosting."

Nikki shut her eyes tightly. Memories of last year's birthday— all but forgotten in the shock of finding herself pregnant—made her feel more like giving thanks than wishing for anything new.

What to wish for now? Looking for ideas, she opened her eyes and scanned the group that gathered before the wide bay window, Lake Michigan stretched out blue and peaceful far below.

Jeff, she thought, glancing at his short, dark hair, at the deep blue eyes she loved. *I could wish that he'd care about me again. I was so stupid last year, I didn't give him a second thought. And now—*

"Nikki!" Gram reminded her. "The wax!"

But most of all, that things would be okay with my mother. And Dad, she added hastily, trying not to look too obviously at Rachel, who stood at the back of the group, her face pale and drawn, the confusion back in her eyes.

Nikki gulped in a huge breath and blew hard. The candles went dark; everyone laughed and applauded.

"Speech! Speech!" Abby and Adam yelled. As the group sang "Happy Birthday," the twins added parts that made Marlene Allen, their mother, frown pointedly at them. Carl, their father, made a quick cutting motion across his neck with one horizontal forefinger; the kids quickly reverted to the traditional version of the song, grins shrinking.

There were presents to unwrap then. There was a pink nightshirt from Keesha that read, "I'm Tired, I'm Grouchy, Leave Me Alone!" From Arleta, ardent fan of old movies, came a video of *The Preacher's Wife*. From her grandparents and the Allens and Aunt Marta, who was now busy handing out slices of lemon cake, there was a beautiful set of luggage. The pieces were made of a buttery-soft, blue leather Nikki wanted to run her hands over again and again.

"For all the trips we've been taking. May there be many more in the future," Marta said, and set a huge piece of cake on the table in front of her niece.

"Hey, I'll never eat all that," Nikki said. "At least I shouldn't."

From her mother, there was a gift certificate for a free makeover and $50 worth of makeup at Merle Norman Cosmetics. Rachel seemed hardly to notice Nikki's thank-you.

By the time Nikki got to Jeff's present, the party had broken into different conversations. His package was small, a tiny metallic-pink giftbag with pink and gray patterned tissue paper gathered gently in the opening. Jeff, who had been standing quietly beside her grandfather throughout the singing and candle-blowing, moved to her side. He leaned down a little to speak to her, and Nikki caught the sweet scent of his cologne. "Hope you like it, Nik."

She pulled out a thin box. Inside lay a narrow chain bracelet, slender and shining, the gold surprisingly heavy between her fingers. "Oh, Jeff, this is *gorgeous*." She looked up into his dark blue eyes and thought how quickly at least one of her wishes was coming true. "Thank you so much, but I don't think you should have—"

"Hey, old friends are important, right?" Jeff said. "Here, let me put it on for you. It'll look great with that outfit." He set his cake plate down, then looked up in alarm. "Of course, the outfit looks great by itself," he hurried to add. "I didn't mean it needed anything else." For a second, there was a flash of the old, awkward Jeff, and Nikki smiled.

"I didn't think you'd have time to buy presents at freshman orientation," she teased.

"Believe me," he answered, "we don't have time to do anything fun at orientation! I'd much rather be here."

I like the sound of that, she thought, feeling a little surge of pleasure at the idea that he might prefer her company to the University of Michigan. "You don't like it there?" she asked.

"No, it's not that. I *do* like it. But I was ready for a break. By the time you finish all the testing garbage and the sessions about how to study and where to find the dining hall, you're up to here—" he passed his hand, ruler-flat, under his chin"—with lectures. And plenty ready for a Labor Day break. I have to admit, though, the social stuff every night is kind of fun."

Nikki's heart sank at the picture of Jeff meeting new girls every night. *How many could there be at orientation, anyway?* she wondered. *Hundreds? Thousands?* She didn't want to think about that. "Well, anyway, this really is beautiful," she said again, moving her arm so that the slender chain slid down to circle her wrist. "You picked exactly the kind of bracelet I love."

Jeff shrugged. "You can thank Carly for that."

"Carly? But she's at the clinic."

"She picked this out before she left, from one of those catalogs she's always getting in the mail. We figured she'd know your taste better than me, and she wanted to get something special, to kind of thank you for helping her in Virginia."

Nikki looked down at the floor, hoping the disappointment didn't show on her face. "Oh. That was . . . really . . . thoughtful of her. And you."

Jeff smiled and picked up his plate. "But I do have a surprise for you, tomorrow, if you can come over for brunch about 10."

Her spirits rose a little. "A surprise? Really?"

"Well, yeah. I mean, it's sort of a surprise—sort of something I want your opinion on, you know?"

She opened her mouth to question him further, but the twins

crowded close to get a look at the bracelet. "Oooh, Nikki," Abby cooed. "Jeff gave you *that?*" She gave Adam a look that was obviously supposed to carry great significance.

Adam responded by thumping Jeff on the back. "Good choice for an old guy," he told his big brother.

Keesha bumped shoulders with Nikki as she reached for the bowl of mixed nuts, and Nikki thanked her for the nightshirt.

"Yeah, I figured you'd like that. I couldn't think what else to get you. Then I remembered you laughing about Carly's shirt, the one that said the same thing." Keesha's dark index finger poked among the peanuts to find the cashews. "Listen, can you come over tomorrow for a while, Nik?"

Nikki hesitated. "I don't know, Keesha. Maybe." She glanced at Jeff, making sure he had moved far enough away to be out of hearing distance, then leaned closer to Keesha. "Jeff said he wants to surprise me with something tomorrow."

Keesha opened her eyes wide and waggled her eyebrows, but Nikki made a face, warning her silently not to say anything Jeff might hear. "Maybe I can come over after that," she whispered, then returned to a normal tone, as though they were carrying on a conversation about the weather. "How's Serena? And what've you been up to while I was in Virginia?"

Keesha and Nikki had become friends by default the year before, the only two girls who were pregnant at Howellsville High School. Whenever Nikki had needed to talk, she knew she could count on Keesha, who always reminded her that, when it came to having babies, she'd been there, done that, and, as Keesha always added with a smirk, even had the T-shirt.

Nikki grinned involuntarily, remembering the oversized hot-pink sweatshirt Keesha had worn, with huge black letters across the chest proclaiming BABY and a wide black arrow pointing down at Keesha's bulging stomach, as if there could be any confusion on that point.

Nikki knew things had changed for Keesha after Serena was born, though. Keesha's family couldn't help with the baby as much as she'd expected, and she found herself in the role of a stay-at-home mom at a time when she most wanted to be out with friends. Nikki had watched Keesha's boredom and unhappiness grow through the spring and early summer.

"I want you to come over so I can show you what I've been doing," Keesha was saying. "My brother bought a computer, and he lets me use it as much as I want when he's at work. I met some people on the Web, and—" She spread her hands wide. "I don't know how to explain it, Nikki. It's like I have all these friends now. It's like a whole new world."

Grandpa reached between them for a handful of nuts. "I couldn't help hearing what you said, Keesha. You're into the Web now, too?"

Keesha looked at him, surprised. "What do you mean, 'too'? Don't tell me *you're* online, Mr. Nobles!"

"Well, sure! You think I'm too old or something?" Grandpa grinned at her. "I kept hearing the Internet was such a great tool for doing research, so I signed up, but I must be doing something wrong. I'm writing an article on plankton, but when I got online to search for information, the darned thing told me there were six million matches, give or take a few hundred thousand, that I had to sort through."

Grandpa set his empty cake plate on the table and accepted a glass of soda from Arleta. "I have this feeling there's a whole lot more information out there about plankton than I'll ever want to know."

Keesha shook her head. "You've definitely gotta learn how to narrow your search, Mr. Nobles."

"Sounds good, if I had a clue how to do it. Anyway, that was just the beginning of my troubles, Keesha. I figured I'd get in touch with my old friend Bill Schall, a marine biologist out in Oregon who does a lot of research. He gave me his e-mail address once, but when I needed it this morning, I couldn't find it. So I called him to get his address again, and we ended up talking on the phone for two and a half hours. So when you add the phone bill to the fee each month for the Internet, I figure it'd be cheaper for me to drive to the nearest ocean and do original research." Grandpa's mouth wore an exaggerated frown, but his eyes sparkled with laughter as he detailed his computer troubles to Keesha. She, in turn, was eager to share what she knew.

"Well, listen, that's something I can show you in no time—how to look up people's e-mail addresses, how to put them in your e-mail address book so you don't have to remember them, stuff like that."

Grandpa turned to Jeff and Nikki. "I think I'll sign up Keesha to be my personal Internet tutor on the spot. She sounds like a pro to me."

Keesha choked on her mouthful of cashews and waved his compliment away. "Pro? *Right!* I've been online for two whole weeks now."

"That puts you a week and six days ahead of me. We're going to have my first lesson right now, I believe." He looked at Keesha questioningly, and she nodded.

"Lead the way! It'll take me about 10 minutes to tell you everything I know."

"Cool!" Adam said, gulping the last of his soda and grabbing a handful of nuts so he and Abby could follow. Jeff trailed the group toward Grandpa's study.

Nikki went to where Rachel stood alone at the bay window, staring out over Lake Michigan, an untouched cup of coffee, still steaming faintly, in her hands. "Mother? *Mother!*"

Rachel turned slightly and stared at Nikki, her face impassive.

"Are you coming to the study with us?"

Rachel gave a barely perceptible shake of her head and turned back toward the window.

The gnawing feeling in Nikki's stomach started again. "Why don't you come with us?" she whispered. "Maybe it'll get your mind off whatever's wrong, just for now."

The result was unnerving. Without so much as turning her head or looking at Nikki, Rachel set her cup on the window sill with such force that coffee splashed onto the white-painted wood. Her well-trained singer's voice was completely under control, and low enough that no one but Nikki could hear, but laced with unmistakable fury. *"I told you not to mention this until I'm ready!"* Nikki shot a glance around the room to make sure no one else had heard, then followed the others to the study.

Grandpa's book-lined study, at the front of the house across from the living room, had always been one of Nikki's favorite places. The stamp of his personality was evident on everything in the room, from the still-open Bible and theology book on the brown leather couch, to the square, yellow sticky notes that covered the green glass shade of the desk lamp.

Nikki laughed to see that the little yellow squares had now spread to the side and frame of the computer monitor as well. As her grandfather settled into his chair and switched on the computer, the rest of them crowded around the desk. He gestured toward the notes that seemed to bristle everywhere. "That's what they'll put on my tombstone, I imagine," he said as they waited for the computer to boot up. "Death by stickies."

He worked his way slowly, deliberately, through the steps of connecting to the Internet, and Nikki thought how, under other circumstances, she had always loved to watch him work. Never in a hurry, Roger Nobles simply faced any task before him calmly and did it well.

Tonight, though, it was almost impossible for Nikki to be patient. She knew that, until everyone was gone, Rachel would hold her secret locked inside, and keep Nikki feeling as though she stood on the edge of a precipice.

With effort, Nikki turned her attention back to her grandfather. His hair, now almost completely white, and the deep creases around his mouth should have made him look old, by any standards. But his bright blue eyes, so intent on what he was doing, overshadowed the marks of age. She watched his lips move, as he spoke aloud each word he typed.

"You shouldn't do that, Mr. Nobles!" Keesha exclaimed.

The older man looked up innocently. "I shouldn't do what, Keesha?"

"Say your password out loud that way."

"OldBio? Why, that just stands for 'old biologist.' "

Keesha rolled her eyes and sighed as though the situation were hopeless. *"That's* what you're not supposed to say, Mr. Nobles. You're not supposed to let anyone know your password! They could get into all your private files and stuff."

Roger Nobles laughed. "Oh, you mean my closely-guarded, top-secret information on plankton? Keesha, at my age I *have* to tell people my password. If I don't, how will I find out what it is when I forget it?"

Keesha gave a loud snort of exasperation. "All the same, you better change it, Mr. Nobles, 'cause now we all know it."

"Well," Grandpa said, speaking slowly as he tapped in the characters of a Web address, "from what I hear, that's one of the lesser dangers of being online."

Keesha looked at the ceiling and laughed. "Oh, go on! People are always making such a big deal about that. I think the worst thing would be having somebody else read all my e-mails."

"My dad says you can get in a lot of trouble if you give out your name and address," Abby piped up, her big eyes serious. "He says you can get hurt."

Watching the homepage that was materializing on the screen, Keesha waved a casual hand. "Listen, Abby, you just gotta be smart. Sure, you can't go giving out information to every person you meet. But after you write back and forth for a while, you can tell what a person's like—whether you can trust them or not."

Keesha leaned forward, one hand on the back of Grandpa's chair, the other pointing to one section of the screen. "Click there, Mr. Nobles, on that word that's underlined."

Nikki was tapping her foot impatiently long before Keesha's 10-minute lesson turned into an hour. Even the twins disappeared after half an hour or so. Jeff and Keesha were intent on the screen before them, however, answering Grandpa's questions and showing him new sites he could access on the Internet. They didn't even notice when Nikki finally decided she could stand it no longer and headed off in the direction of the kitchen, hoping to find her mother alone and more willing to talk.

❦ *Three* ❧

IN THE KITCHEN, the counters gleamed and the dishwasher hummed sedately. Nikki heard voices from the screened porch, where she found her grandmother and Marlene Allen on the porch swing. Her mother and Aunt Marta sat in the white wicker rockers facing the swing. Arleta stood by the screen door, one hand on the frame as though ready to leave.

Seeing Nikki, Marta gestured to the empty lawn chair beside her. "We've got a spot right here for you, Birthday Lady."

Nikki could see she'd have no chance to talk to her mother alone, but it would have been rude to leave then. She slid into the chair and thanked them all once again for the presents.

The sun had set while she'd been in Grandpa's study, and the sky over Lake Michigan was foggy gray now, touched with a thin line of rose at the horizon. The evening air, fragrant with the scent of Gram's late-blooming honeysuckle, was still warm against Nikki's bare arms. As usually happened when they were together, Arleta took over the conversation.

"WHY, NIKKI, HONEY, IT'S SO GOOD TO SEE YOU! YOU'RE LOOKING BETTER THAN EVER. IT'S JUST SUCH A SHAME ABOUT CARLY, ISN'T IT? I WAS DOWN AT THE DRUGSTORE LAST NIGHT AND MABEL WIERENGA WAS TELLING ME YOU WERE BACK FROM YOUR TRIP WITH MARTA. SHE TOLD ME

19

ALL ABOUT CARLY HAVING THIS EATING DISORDER."

Nikki squirmed in the lawn chair. *How can she bring that up, right in front of Carly's mom? Computers may be boring, but I should have stayed with Keesha and Jeff and Grandpa.*

It wasn't that Arleta was a terrible person or anything, Nikki thought. The woman always had been there for Gram, especially after the stroke. Arleta had brought hundreds of dishes—salads, casseroles, pies, cookies, homemade bread—to the blue clapboard house over the past year.

So how come every time I see her, I want to run the other way? Nikki thought. The word *outspoken* came to mind, but didn't seem to cover it. Maybe it was the fact that Arleta was a walking, breathing encyclopedia of current events, thanks to her work at the Rosendale library where she read all the daily newspapers. Or the way she went on and on about Arnold, her policeman son, and the extensive collection of old movies she lovingly tended at the library.

Or maybe, Nikki thought, *it's just hard to be around someone who's usually right—and knows it.*

"NIKKI," Arleta continued, "I ESPECIALLY WANTED TO TALK TO YOU ABOUT SOMETHING. DID YOU KNOW WE'VE STARTED A ROSENDALE CHAPTER OF 'WOMENS' OUT-REACH'? "

Nikki sat silently, knowing Arleta almost never waited for an answer to her questions.

"WE'RE VERY CONCERNED ABOUT WHAT'S GOING ON AROUND HERE. YOU KNOW ABOUT THE TWO SHOOTINGS IN HOWELLSVILLE THIS PAST WINTER, AND THE ROBBERIES IN MUSKEGON AND THE—" she lowered her voice, looking sideways at the floor as she said the word in a near whisper—"*rapes.*"

Arleta shuddered, then went on. "WHY, FIVE YEARS AGO, WE DIDN'T EVEN LOCK OUR DOORS! MABEL WIERENGA HAD TO GET A NEW KEY MADE LAST YEAR. IT WAS SO LONG SINCE SHE USED HERS, SHE COULDN'T FIND IT. WEST MICHIGAN IS GETTING MORE AND MORE LIKE THE OTHER SIDE OF THE STATE. NEXT THING WE KNOW, WE'LL HAVE GANGS AND DRUG DEALERS IF WE DON'T TURN THINGS AROUND."

The veiled reference to Detroit made Nikki smile a little. As long as she'd known Arleta, the 'other side of the state'—specifically Detroit—had represented the very embodiment of evil in the woman's mind.

"SO WE'RE HOSTING A SPECIAL TEA FOR ALL THE WOMEN IN TOWN NEXT WEEK, INCLUDING HIGH SCHOOL AND COLLEGE AGE GIRLS. NOT TO TALK ABOUT CRIME, OF COURSE, BUT TO TALK ABOUT GOD AND HOW HE CAN CHANGE PEOPLE. WE'RE BRINGING IN A SPEAKER FROM GRAND RAPIDS, BUT WE'VE ALSO ASKED A FEW LOCAL PEOPLE TO TELL THEIR OWN STORIES ABOUT HOW GOD CHANGED THEM. BRIEFLY, OF COURSE. BEFORE THE MAIN PART OF THE MEETING BEGINS."

Nikki tried to keep her thoughts on what Arleta was saying, wondering vaguely when the older woman would get around to actually inviting her. So Arleta's next words came as a shock.

"WE'D LIKE YOU TO BE ONE OF THE ONES TO TELL YOUR STORY, NIKKI. WOULD YOU DO THAT?"

"*My* story?" Nikki squeaked, sitting bolt upright on her chair. "What story? You don't mean—about me having the baby?"

Arleta nodded vigorously, her silver-white hair bouncing with each nod.

Nikki shook her head so hard that it began to ache. "No way! I mean, I'm sorry, Arleta, I don't mean to be rude—but I couldn't possibly do that. Get up in front of people and talk about the most private thing in my whole—no! I can't!"

Arleta smiled, but in a way that said she had no intention of giving up. She pushed open the screen door. "WELL, I'VE GOT TO GET ON HOME NOW, BUT YOU TAKE SOME TIME TO THINK ABOUT IT, NIKKI. MAYBE I CAME ON A LITTLE STRONG. PEOPLE HAVE TOLD ME THAT I SOMETIMES DO THAT, THOUGH I CAN'T SAY I SEE IT MYSELF."

Nikki glanced at Arleta, wondering if the woman could actually be making a joke, but Arleta appeared to be dead serious. "WE CAN TALK MORE TOMORROW, WHEN I COME BACK."

Aunt Marta grinned as Arleta disappeared around the corner of the house. "Except for the white hair, I don't think she's changed one iota since I was a little girl."

Gram smiled in return and nodded. Soon conversation between the two of them and Marlene Allen hummed around Nikki. But she was far away, sorting memories from 18 years of summers spent here in her grandparents' house. They were peaceful memories, for the most part. *If you don't count last year.*

Those were memories she tried not to think of often. She'd sat here on this same porch a year ago, pregnant and terrified and confused beyond words. But until then her grandparents' house had always been her sanctuary, a shelter from the continual storm of life with her parents back in Ohio.

She'd thought this house would be her sanctuary once again, now that Evan was born and placed with a good family. The pain of missing him, yearning to be with him, never went completely away, but the adoption was working out well. Nikki knew she'd made the right decision for him.

But now, just when she'd been congratulating herself on finally getting her life back to normal, some new trouble was brewing. Uneasiness hung thick in the air like humidity before a summer storm. And Rachel was the one who had brought it here.

Nikki glanced at her mother, who sat silently in the white wicker rocker. One arm rested on the back, the long, manicured fingers absently twisting a strand of permed hair dyed the color of clover honey. Rachel would never stand for the streaks of gray her younger sister Marta took so for granted.

Sometimes it seemed to Nikki that Rachel was all about hiding—hiding her gray hair, hiding every flaw of her complexion under porcelain makeup, hiding her real feelings behind sharp criticism of others. She'd tried to force Nikki to hide her pregnancy by getting an abortion.

And now she's hiding something else, some trouble she'd brought to the one place in the whole world that felt safe. Nikki felt like a country invaded.

By eleven o'clock that night, only family remained at the blue clapboard house. Aunt Marta finally got up from the white wicker rocker, stretching her arms high above her head and yawning. "I am absolutely beat," she said, the words distorted by the yawn. She held out one hand toward the porch swing where Gram sat. "I'll give you a hand with those therapy exercises if you come upstairs now. Otherwise, I can't promise I'll be awake for more than 15 more minutes."

Gram was glad to accept Marta's offer. After another round of happy birthdays, the two of them disappeared through the kitchen doorway.

Once Nikki and her mother were alone, Nikki found herself unsure how to begin the conversation. She moved to the porch swing, always her favorite spot, and stretched out among the flowered pillows piled there, setting the swing moving with nervous pushes of her bare toes against the wooden floorboards. *May as well get comfortable for whatever's coming.* She tried to make light of her fear as she waited for her mother to say something. *Kind of like a prisoner getting one last good meal before he gets bumped off.*

She strained to see Rachel's face in the dark, but could make out only a black silhouette against the gray of the lake beyond. Finally she could wait no longer.

"Mother! Are you going to tell me what's going on now?"

The wicker rocker creaked as Rachel shifted in her chair, but still she said nothing.

"Come *on*, Mother. Why didn't Dad come with you?"

When Rachel finally answered, Nikki was shocked at the naked pain in her voice. "Your father . . ." Rachel sighed, then began again. "Your father left. Last weekend."

Back. Forward. Back. Forward. For a long moment, the only reality was the sway of the swing, the feel of the warm night air flowing against Nikki's face.

Did you have a bigger fight than usual? It was the first thing that came to her mind. For Nikki, memories of her parents had always included arguments.

"He left?" Nikki's mouth had suddenly gone dry, and she licked her lips before she could say more. "Like he's gone away to—work on things? So they'll be better between you two?"

The bitterness in Rachel's voice was unmistakable. "Hardly. That would be too much to expect from someone who hasn't looked his own problems in the face for 46 years, wouldn't it? No, Nicole. Your father is gone. He wants a divorce."

Nikki had known that, whatever was wrong, it was bad. But not this bad.

She sat up slowly and pulled her knees against her chest, circling them with her arms, trying to hold herself together. "What do you mean, 'gone'? I mean, where is he right now?"

Rachel hesitated again. Nikki could almost feel her struggling to force the words out. When she finally did, her voice was back to its usual cadence—clipped, precise, void of emotion. "Your father's at a townhouse he rented over in Mountain View."

It was too much for Nikki to make sense of all at once, so she fastened on the first thing that flashed through her mind. *Mountain View.* Everyone always joked about the name of the high-class, highest-priced neighborhood Millbrook, Ohio, could boast. There wasn't a mountain within a hundred miles, and barely a hill that deserved the name.

Nikki tried to picture her father living in a townhouse there, alone. *What is he doing for furniture? For dishes?* She wondered what he'd taken from the house.

She hugged herself more tightly, trying to ignore the sudden, unexpected stab of loss. She'd been gone for a year from that house, now. If someone had asked, she would have said she'd never felt at home there anyway. Not like she did here, at her grandparents'. So why did the thought of her father, alone in a bare townhouse, hurt this bad? Why did it matter so much?

She wanted to yell at Rachel, demand to know what her mother had done to drive him away. But Rachel was still talking.

"Apparently there's . . ." Nikki could see the dark silhouette of Rachel's hands moving in the air, struggling to express the words she could hardly mouth. "There's . . . another woman involved. He met her last year, after we found out you were pregnant."

Another woman involved. Nikki's mind probed the words as cautiously as she would overturn a starfish on the beach with her bare toe.

Now it was the idea of Rachel, alone in the Millbrook house, crying, that filled her mind. Slowly, Nikki tried to form a picture of her father with a woman other than her mother—laughing with her, eating meals with her, kissing her.

Suddenly Nikki wanted to jump in the blue Mazda and drive fast—way over the speed limit—till she could pound her fist on the front door of her father's townhouse in snooty Mountain View. She pictured how his face would look when he opened the door, when she screamed her feelings at him. Nikki sat up straight and pushed the thoughts away, tried not to feel the hard, metallic taste of fury in her mouth.

She wet her lips again and asked, "What are you going to do now?"

There was another sigh from Rachel. "Stay here for a while, I suppose. Until I decide what to do. Of course, I have to get back to Ohio to teach soon, but I could take a week of personal time if I have to."

That explains the suitcases, Nikki thought. Aloud, she asked, "Have you told Gram and Grandpa yet? Any of this?"

"I thought you should be the first to know."

And then Rachel did what Nikki dreaded more than anything else, what she'd seen her mother do only one other time—after the stroke, when Gram had slipped into a coma in the hospital.

Rachel covered her face with her hands and began to sob.

Nikki watched her for a moment, filled with remorse. The thought occurred to her that she could put her arms around her mother and comfort her, but it was fleeting. For other mothers and daughters, like Carly and Marlene Allen, or Aunt Marta and Gram, a hug at this point would be as natural as breathing. But Nikki couldn't even remember the last time she had hugged her mother. She realized, with a wave of helplessness, that she didn't have a clue what to do.

At the same time, to her shame, she found herself wondering if it was too late to get away from Rachel and call Jeff. The need to tell someone she was close to was almost overpowering. She automatically glanced toward the watch on her wrist, but couldn't make out the numbers in the dark. Besides, she couldn't just leave, not with her mother sobbing her eyes out this way, right here on the porch.

A kind of quiet panic began to spread inside Nikki, shattering the edges of her calm like breaking thin ice over a dry puddle. She wanted to ask a million questions, and she didn't want to ask any. She would have to look the situation in the face, she knew. Grapple with it.

But not yet. Not as long as she could hold it off. Nikki stabbed her toe against the floor and set the swing in motion, fast.

❧ *Four* ❧

NIKKI COMPROMISED, FINALLY, by slipping off the swing and going to stand beside her mother's chair, patting her silk-clad shoulder awkwardly. Rachel reached up to take her hand and held on, as though for dear life.

Nikki, unnerved by the sight of the always-sophisticated and in-control Rachel falling apart so completely, cast about for some way to find help. "Mother, don't you want me to go get Gram and Grandpa? And Aunt Marta?"

Rachel sniffed hard and brushed at her wet cheeks with her free hand. "Not—when I'm like this. I'll—tell them—tomorrow." Her breath came in little hiccups from crying, and Nikki listened in amazement. *I thought only kids did that.*

Eventually the hiccupping stopped and silence settled over them. Only the distant call of a whippoorwill followed them as they finally made their way upstairs, long after everyone else was in bed.

Nikki fled to her room and curled up on the window seat, welcoming the darkness of the room around her. Far out across Lake Michigan the pinpoint lights of a barge crawled along the horizon. In the yard below her window the metered rasp of cicadas rose from every tree. Nikki stared and listened, listened and stared, like a detached onlooker, as dry and brittle inside as an autumn leaf.

At last she stumbled toward her bed in the darkness and curled up on the cool cotton sheets. She knew there would be black eye makeup on the pillowcase in the morning if she didn't wash it off now, but the effort was beyond her.

Nikki's sleep was light, unsettled. She surfaced again and again to a state of near-waking, almost as though listening for something. She realized, when she finally woke completely in the pale gray predawn, that what she was listening for was, in some sense, her father. She was waiting for David Sheridan to undo what he'd done, to call up and say, "I must have been out of my mind. Of course I'm coming back. I would never do this to you and your mother."

Nikki threw back the cotton blanket she must have pulled up during the night and swung her legs over the side of the bed. The bedroom door creaked open slightly and Gallie's golden snout poked hopefully around the edge.

Nikki held out her hand to him, beckoning. His tail thumped wildly against the door as he squeezed through the doorway and trotted to her side. She leaned down and hugged the dog's head, breathing in the clean smell of his fur, rubbing her cheek against his softness.

"Want to go for a walk, boy?" she whispered. Gallie wriggled in ecstasy, frantically licking at her face and hands and hair. She made him sit, then dressed quickly in denim shorts and a T-shirt.

In just a few minutes they were outside, entering the dune forest. The tall, stately oaks and graceful aspens seemed to lend some of their stillness to her soul each time she came here. A boardwalk had long ago been built over the ecologically fragile dune, and Nikki climbed it now to her special place at the crest of the hill.

The pre-dawn air was dank and motionless as Nikki ducked under the boardwalk railing and crossed the sandy ground to sit crosslegged beneath the giant oak. Soon a small, tenuous breeze rustled through the treetops, bringing with it the fresh scent of morning—just as the first faint fingers of pale sunlight reached through the forest from behind her, barely warming her skin.

Gallie waited at attention, his dark, moist nose quivering, until he caught the scent of a squirrel and bounded off in hot pursuit.

Nikki lost sight of him in the thick woods that covered the steep dune.

The top branches of the oak in front of and below her framed her view of Lake Michigan. The surface of the water was gray silk, undulating from beneath as swell after gentle swell rolled in toward the shore, never breaking the surface. As the pale sunlight grew stronger, the water gleamed blue, and a gull rose into the air above it, wheeling and crying over the deserted beach.

A lone figure jogged across the sand, his long legs taking the distance easily. Nikki could tell by the gait that it was Jeff. She scrambled to her feet and started to call him, then stopped as she watched him turn to climb the steps toward the houses. The sound of her voice would never carry that far.

She turned and called for Gallie instead, then clattered back down the boardwalk stairs and raced to the yard behind the blue house where she could get Jeff's attention.

"Jeff!" she said as he came into view over the cliff, keeping her voice quiet enough to not wake anyone inside. He turned, surprised, and came toward her.

"Hey, what are you doing up so early? I didn't think I'd see you till 10." His voice turned teasing. "Don't tell me—you decided it was time you finally saw a sunrise, right? So what'd you think of it?"

The look on her face squelched his attempt at humor, and concern replaced his grin.

Under his scrutiny, she realized with a sinking feeling that she hadn't even looked in the mirror yet this morning, and the remains of last night's makeup must be all over her face. But there was nothing she could do about it now. Besides, Jeff had already seen her at her worst, in the hospital just after she'd given birth to Evan.

If he still cared about her after that, she knew she was safe with him now. *If*, her mind emphasized, but she pushed the thought away.

"Can you come for a walk with me, Jeff?" She took in his T-shirt blotched with sweat, his face flushed from running. "I mean, right now? I need to talk to you."

Jeff dried his face with the bottom half of his T-shirt, then nodded. "Sure. What's wrong, Nik?"

She didn't answer, just motioned him to follow her back toward the dune where they could be alone. Nikki sat down on the bottom step of the boardwalk, and Jeff dropped down beside her. She caught herself starting to peel her fingernails, a habit she'd broken only in the past year, and clenched her hands into fists to stop herself. A robin sang from somewhere above, a bright, liquid melody she would have loved at any other time, but right now all her thoughts were concentrated on getting out the words she had to tell Jeff.

"My dad left, Jeff. Left my mother, I mean. She told me last night."

Jeff stopped in the middle of wiping his face again and stared at Nikki, his mouth open. "He *what?*"

"He left her. For another woman. That's why Mother came up here alone. That whole story about coming for my birthday was just a smokescreen. She's got a whole trunk full of luggage because she's staying here. She just hasn't told anybody yet, except me."

Jeff stared into Nikki's eyes, searching. Then he reached out slowly and pulled her close to him. "I'm so sorry, Nikki."

Nikki sank against his chest. Their nearness reminded her of the year before when they'd sat the same way, the day she'd told him she was pregnant. There had been tears then, and release in the tears, because she could finally tell someone her secret.

This time, though, no tears came, and no release. She simply leaned against him silently, her heart like lead. *The only good thing in this whole mess is being close to Jeff again*, she thought, *having things back the way they used to be.*

They sat that way until Gallie dashed back from his squirrel chase, full of pride, wagging his feathery tail madly. He burrowed his snout under Jeff's arm, trying to get at Nikki. Jeff pushed him away gently. "Not now, boy. Go on, go get some more chipmunks, or squirrels, or whatever you were after."

At last Nikki moved away a little and sat up straight. She

brushed the dark curls back off her face. "I guess it's crazy for me to be this upset."

Jeff looked at her, frowning. "Crazy? What are you talking about? What else could you be but upset?"

She shrugged one shoulder. "Well, my family isn't like—like *your* family, that's for sure. I've never been very close to my parents, not like you are. Especially after last year, when I had Evan and all. But still, somehow, I always kind of—*hoped*, you know? And prayed. That things would change, that we'd be a—a *real* family. But now—"

Jeff nodded slowly, his head tilted slightly to one side, the way he always sat when he was listening intently.

Nikki gave a short laugh. "I guess that idea's out the window, huh?"

Still Jeff was silent. Nikki looked at him and raised her eyebrows. "Well? Got any great advice for me?"

Even as she said the words, she could feel the flush of embarrassment move up her neck and spread across her face. She felt as if she were seeing her family through Jeff's eyes, and she cringed at how it must look. *Jeff's parents would never even dream of doing this kind of thing. They'd never blow it this way.*

When he finally spoke, Jeff's voice did little to dispel her shame. "I'm trying to think of something even remotely intelligent to say here, Nik, something that would help. But I'm not coming up with anything. Except that praying for your parents is really important right now. But that sounds so trite, like a cop-out."

Disappointment welled up strongly in Nikki's chest. She'd expected more than that from Jeff.

∞

By the time Nikki had showered and dressed for brunch—picking shorts and a Mickey Mouse T-shirt that had once made Jeff laugh—the temperature had dropped 10 degrees. A bank of thick, gray clouds had swept in across Lake Michigan, covering Rosendale like a felt blanket. From her seat on the porch swing, Nikki watched the clouds spread their darkness and thought how it suddenly looked and felt like fall. Shivering, she remembered that school was starting in just three days.

Nikki had been on pins and needles for two hours now, playing a waiting game with the clock. She felt sure that as soon as Rachel came downstairs, she would break the news about Nikki's dad to the family—and she didn't want to be around when that happened. Hearing it shared with others would solidify it somehow, make it real—and she couldn't bear to think what the news would do to her grandparents. But she couldn't turn up at Allens' before 10, either. Finally, just before the hall clock began to chime 10 o'clock, Nikki got up and hurried through the kitchen. "I'm going to Allens' for brunch," she said in the direction of Aunt Marta and Grandma, who were unloading the dishwasher. "Tell Mother I'm sorry I missed her, and I'll see her later, okay?" She winced as she said the words, realizing how relieved she was to escape.

She hurried across the driveway, wondering only vaguely about the gleaming black Saturn SC2 parked behind Allens' car, realizing they must have invited someone else to brunch, too. Nikki gave the Allens' kitchen door a courtesy knock, pushed it open—and stopped dead.

Jeff stood in the middle of the kitchen, a dark silhouette against the wall of windows looking out on Lake Michigan. Beside him stood another silhouette, one Nikki didn't recognize.

The two figures moved around the counter then, and Nikki could see clearly the stranger's long, blond hair, her immaculate khaki pants and pink silk T-shirt, her stunning figure, and flawless face. *Even her smile is perfect*, Nikki thought, as she looked at all those even, white teeth sparkling at her.

Too late Nikki remembered that she should smile back. Her mind was stuck on the fact that, in the face of this girl's totally gorgeous outfit, Nikki's Mickey Mouse T-shirt now seemed ridiculous.

Nikki was still working on remembering how to smile when Jeff stepped forward, beaming. "This is Shannon, Nik. This is what—I mean *who*—I wanted you to meet." He reached back and pulled the girl's hand gently, urging her forward to stand beside him. "Shannon, this is Nikki Sheridan. Nikki's like, one of my oldest friends in the world. We've both been coming here to Lake Michigan every summer for as long as I can remember. I couldn't wait to have you meet her."

Then Jeff, who seemed more enthusiastic than Nikki had seen him for a long time, turned to face her. "Nik, this is Shannon Schwartz. We met the first day of orientation at U of M. She's studying to be a vet, so we'll be in a lot of the same courses together for the first couple years."

I'm delighted for you, Nikki thought, feeling anger and hurt swirl together in the pit of her stomach. *How convenient that you have all those classes together. That's just great, Jeff. Did I mention I'm delighted for you?*

Minutes later Nikki was sitting directly across the table from Shannon, thinking she'd seen enough dazzling displays of those perfectly white teeth to last a lifetime. Shannon was a smiler, no doubt about it. She smiled as she told everyone how helpful Jeff had been, showing her around the huge U of M campus. She smiled as she answered Carl and Marlene's polite questions about her family, explaining that her father was also a vet and had started taking her along to his clinic at the age of eight to help hold kittens and puppies still while he gave them shots, and that her mother had put a successful teaching career on hold to be at home while raising Shannon.

Great, Nikki thought. *That's just great. Shannon comes from a family like Jeff's—picture perfect. How am I supposed to compete with that?*

Shannon, meanwhile, was demonstrating her ability to smile even while she ate. Nikki couldn't figure out how the girl managed to look so gorgeous and poised while she did it. *If I showed that many teeth while I chewed, breakfast would be all over Mickey Mouse's face.*

Eventually Shannon turned to Nikki and asked, "What about you? Are you from around here?"

Nikki's face felt strangely tight as she forced her own lips to turn up in a completely unnatural smile and answered. The tight feeling didn't go away as they talked, or even as they ate their way through Marlene Allen's favorite breakfast casserole, made with eggs and cheese and sausage. It was a dish Nikki had eaten a thousand times before and raved about.

Funny, she thought, *this casserole doesn't taste nearly as good as it used to. In fact, it doesn't seem to have any taste at all.*

After two hours of sheer torture, Nikki escaped to her grandparents' house as soon as she decently could. Jeff had invited Nikki along to show Shannon the beach, but Nikki had stammered out the first excuse that came to mind. "I really need to—to help my mother. She's not all unpacked yet."

I hope that's not a lie, she thought as she said her goodbyes and started back across the gravel drive. *But at this point, I don't really care.*

No way would she be part of a happy little trio on the beach. The beach was *their* place—Nikki's and Jeff's—the beach and the dune and the pier. So what was he doing, taking another girl there?

But even as she asked, Nikki knew. The look in Jeff's eyes when he talked to Shannon, the excitement in his voice when he introduced her—it was all too clear what he was doing.

No wonder he acted so strange this morning on the dune, she thought. All the time she'd been pouring her heart out about the mess her family was in, he'd probably been thinking about Shannon, the smiler. And about her perfect family.

Nikki let the screen door slam behind her, feeling as though her whole world had come tumbling down in the last two days. *First my parents, now Jeff.*

Nikki put in an appearance at lunch—but said she was too full to eat. The truth was that she could no longer remember what—or if—she'd eaten at the Allens'.

It was obvious from the conversation that Rachel hadn't told Gram and Grandpa and Marta the news yet. Nikki's eyes met her mother's over the glasses while the others talked. Nikki raised her eyebrows ever so slightly, and Rachel gave a barely perceptible shake of her head in return.

What are you waiting for, Mother? Nikki wanted to scream. *Get it over with, already!*

It was only one o'clock when Nikki marched up the sidewalk to Keesha's house and slammed her hand against the doorbell. The day was crawling by in slow motion—slow, agonizing motion.

"You will never, *ever* believe what happened this morning!" Nikki burst out as soon as Keesha opened the door.

Keesha's deep-brown eyes widened at her vehemence. "Whoa! Sounds like major stuff, Nik. You better come on back to my room. We'll have to talk quiet 'cuz Serena just went down for her nap." Nikki followed her back down the hall, then plopped herself down, crosslegged, on the foot of Keesha's bed and faced her friend who sat in the same position at the head.

"Keesha! He's done nothing but act sweet to me for two days, ever since I got back—"

"Wait! Who are we talkin' about here? You mean Jeff?"

"Of course, *Jeff*. Jeff the traitor! Keesha, I thought everything was back to the way it used to be. He liked me for ages. I mean, I know things got a little mixed-up when I was pregnant, but I thought we'd worked that out, you know? From the way he'd been acting, I was sure we did."

Suddenly Nikki felt tears running down her cheeks. She dashed them away with angry hands.

Keesha leaned forward. "So what did he do that's so awful?"

"He met a girl at U of M. She lives close around here somewhere, so he asked her to come and meet his family and *me*. This morning, for breakfast!"

Keesha's lips pursed as she thought. Then she said, "He asked her here after only a *week* at U of M with her? This is not good, babe."

"Tell me about it! It's a total disaster. He kept talking about how he had this surprise he couldn't wait to share, and how he wanted my opinion on something because we've been friends for so long and—"

"Wait a minute, Nik. He was saying that to you, and all the time he had another girl?"

Nikki nodded, then pulled her knees up to her chin and wiped her wet cheeks against her forearms.

Keesha made a face, grabbed a box of tissues from the nightstand, and shoved it the length of the bed toward her. "Here I thought Jeff was such a great guy last year, you know, taking me to the hospital in the snowstorm and all that," Keesha declared. "Turns out he's just another self-centered jerk, huh?"

Even as she listened to Keesha, Nikki heard another, much smaller, voice in her head. *A jerk? What did Jeff actually say that misled you?* She thought about the bracelet. Jeff had been honest about the fact that Carly had picked it out, that Carly wanted Nikki to have something special for helping her in Virginia.

And he hadn't actually *said* he liked her again. He'd just acted like the old Jeff, kind and sweet and attentive and . . . and she'd assumed. Too much, apparently.

For a second, just a split second, her feelings hung in the balance, and she almost admitted to herself that perhaps this was *her* mistake. But the pain was too intense. Jeff *was* a jerk. Just like the other guys. Like T.J., who had gotten her pregnant. And worst of all—just like her father.

The conversation went on for half an hour or so, until Nikki noticed Keesha glancing furtively—and repeatedly—at the clock radio on the bedside table. Nikki lost her temper and her words dripped with sarcasm. "Keesha, that's the third time you've looked at the clock. Am I keeping you from something important?"

Keesha blew out a huff of air through pursed lips. "You are in some mood, girl! As a matter of fact, I need to make sure my nails are done before tonight. It sounds crazy, but once Serena gets up, there's no way I can do them. I get the polish on, but they never get time to dry before I have to feed her or change her or pick her up, you know?" She slid off the bed and gathered everything she needed for her nails from the dresser and brought it back to the bed, rearranging herself. "There! Now I'm all set. Talk away."

Keesha's actions broke the momentum, though, and Nikki suddenly found she didn't want to rehash everything she'd said already. "There's nothing else to tell you. It's just that—well, I had to talk to someone. And there's no one left at home to talk to. They're all upset over—over—some stuff going on with my parents."

Keesha stroked deep blue polish over her long thumbnail in one long, smooth motion. "Oh, I get it. I'm your last resort, right? Wow, I'm honored!"

"Come on, Keesha, you know what I mean."

Keesha held up her thumb and inspected the nail carefully. "What's going on with your parents?"

Nikki groaned inwardly. *Not now,* she thought. She felt drained enough already. There would be time— some other time—to go into that.

"You know what?" Nikki said. "We've talked enough about me for now. Let's talk about *you.* What's going on tonight that you have to do your nails for?"

Keesha was only too glad to talk about herself, but she teased a little first. "Wellllll--"

"Keesha—"

"I don't know if I should say—"

"Fine," Nikki said. She unfolded her legs and began to slide off the bed. "Go ahead and be that way. I come over here with a totally broken heart and you have the chance to help get my mind off it. But do you want to help? No way!" She slid to her feet.

Keesha leaned forward, grabbed the end of Nikki's T-shirt, and tugged her back down. "Don't get yourself in a snit. Wait till I fix this nail I just messed up on your shirt. Then I'll tell you, okay? I was gonna tell you anyway. That's why I asked you to come over here today, not that you remember, with your mind on Jeff and all."

Nikki resumed her cross-legged position and waited while Keesha repaired the top coat on her pinky. When Keesha looked up, her eyes sparkled with excitement. She capped the polish bottle and set it on the bedside table. "Remember I told you I met some people on the Internet? Well, one of them is coming here, tonight. I get to finally meet him in person!"

"Wait a minute! Let me get this straight. You met some guy on the Internet and he's coming *here*?" Nikki asked.

Keesha grinned. "You got it!"

"But how did you manage that? I mean, people you meet on the

Internet can be from all over the country. All over the world! You mean he actually lives close by?"

Keesha smirked. "Give me credit for a few brains, Nik. You think I'd get involved with someone I can't meet? I'm not that dumb! He lives over by Detroit, and he can get here in three hours. Which means," she added, glancing at the clock radio again, "he's getting ready to leave in just about two hours."

"But Keesha, couldn't that be . . . dangerous? What if he's, like, an ax-murderer or something?"

Keesha rolled her eyes. "Nikki, you are so nuts. I know *all* about Steve—we've been talking every day on the Internet."

"Keesha, people can say *anything* on the Internet. You have no way to prove that what he's telling you is the truth. It could all be absolute *lies!*"

Serena stirred in her crib with a tiny moan and Nikki and Keesha looked at each other in tacit agreement to lower their voices. Keesha got off the bed carefully, silently, and went to check on her baby. When she came back, she spoke in a whisper.

"You're making a big deal out of nothing, Nik. We're just gonna meet and have dinner, that's all. You need to loosen up a little, you know that? I mean, even in our parents' day, people did things called blind dates. This is no different from that.

"Come on in Kurt's room," Keesha continued, "and I'll show you some of the stuff Steve wrote me. In fact, he's got this friend *you* ought to meet." Her face brightened. "Why didn't I think of this before? This is exactly what you need! I'll call Steve and tell him to bring Mitch along and we can all go out together!"

Nikki held up both hands, shaking her head. "Oh, no! You're not getting *me* in on this!"

Keesha looked indignant. Then her scowl turned into a smirk. "I know what's bugging you! You are *such* a racist, you know that? Mitch is white, Nikki, *white*. Perfectly safe. And a perfect doll. Truth is, I almost liked him better than Steve at first, but I didn't want all the complications of dating a white guy again, you know?"

"Oh, brother," Nikki broke in. "Who's being racist now?"

Ignoring her, Keesha reached for the phone. "I'll just call Steve quick, 'cause I'm not sure he'll check his e-mail before he leaves—"

Nikki lunged forward and grabbed her friend's hand. "Stop it, Keesha! I'm not going out with some guy I know nothing about! And I think you're nuts to go out with Steve. When people used to set up blind dates, it was usually friends who did it. People who knew you and cared about whether you were safe or not."

Keesha sat back against the headboard with a sigh. "You can't live in the past, like when people could meet only on the phone or in person." Her eyes narrowed. "Now you listen to me, Nikki Sheridan. What's Jeff gonna think if you let him do this to you? The best thing you can do right now is to meet another guy. And go out with him. Show Jeff Allen he's not the only guy in your life!"

A few minutes later Nikki stood in the doorway of Kurt's room, her arms folded across her chest, watching Keesha boot up her brother's computer. "I'm *not* going out with somebody I never met," Nikki warned.

"For the tenth time, already, I understand. I told you, we won't call him. I'm just gonna turn this on and pull up a couple of Steve's letters. I'll print them out for you and you can see for yourself—he's no spooky Internet stalker!"

Five

IT WAS THREE O'CLOCK by the time Nikki started home from Keesha's. The fog outside had cleared, but it seemed to have moved into her head. Each time her shoes hit the sandy road, her thoughts grew more confused.

Things had moved too fast; that was the problem. Once they had signed on to Keesha's e-mail, they'd found themselves in immediate contact with Mitch. He kept a buddy list and knew the moment Keesha signed on. He'd sent an instant message to ask if she wanted to talk; before Nikki could stop her, Keesha had typed in, "Can't right now, but I have a friend here who's dying to meet you."

Nikki read the message and glared at Keesha, who grinned impishly. "You'll thank me later on," Keesha said, and scooted over to sit on her brother's bed.

Sighing, Nikki sat on the desk chair. "I'm not writing to this guy. I wouldn't have a clue what to say to him, anyhow."

Keesha fell back on the bed dramatically. "Give me a break, Nik! Loosen up a little, would you *please?*" She sat up again and pointed to the message on the screen: *Hey, there—glad to meet you. Any friend of Keesha's is a friend of mine, and all that. I'm Mitch. What's your name?*

Nikki stared at the screen, unmoving.

"He's waiting!" Keesha said.

"I don't care, Keesha! What am I supposed to say to him, any-way?"

Keesha rolled her eyes and reached across Nikki. Her fingers flew over the keys and Nikki watched a new message appear. *I'm glad, too. My name is Nikki. Nicole, actually, but everybody calls me Nikki.*

"Don't send th—" Nikki began, but she was too late. Keesha had hit the "Send" button and was grinning at her like a Cheshire cat.

At least *I didn't get roped into going out with the guy tonight,* Nikki thought, gazing at the lake as she walked. There was a tightness in her stomach when she thought about Keesha's planned meeting with Steve at seven o'clock this evening. *It's not like his letters show any danger signs, but you never know . . .*

On the other hand, maybe she *should* give Mitch a chance. Now that Jeff was going nuts over Shannon the smiler, didn't Nikki deserve to make him a little jealous?

She grinned to herself, feeling the sun's warmth against her shoulders and back. Maybe Keesha was right. Maybe she *did* need to loosen up a little. And maybe the chat she'd just had online with Mitch was the way to do that.

She kicked at a pebble as she walked, watched it roll a few yards, then kicked it again when she caught up with it. She could feel herself walking slower and slower as she neared the Allens' house, reluctant to see the black Saturn in the driveway—or worse yet, to run into the picture-perfect Shannon again.

She turned her mind back to how Keesha had kept saying, "This is like—*fate!* We turn on the computer and find out he's online right now—that's gotta be fate. You better make the most of this."

And it *had* been fun to meet a new guy. Not to mention the fact that it took her mind off a few things she'd rather forget.

As for Mitch—well, he sounded like the farthest thing from an ax-murderer, she had to admit. And kind of romantic, too, which caught her off-guard. He'd asked question after question about what she liked, how she spent her time. Her answers had been reluctant at first, but he'd seemed so interested in getting to know her that she finally gave in and admitted she loved long walks on the beach and sitting by the fireplace on snowy evenings.

I can't believe this, Mitch had written back. *I've been wanting to meet someone like you for a long time. I can tell you're the kind of person I want to get to know, just by how you write.*

He'd seemed much more intelligent than she'd expected. And he knew a lot about music, one of the things she'd said she liked. But she couldn't shake the feeling that there could be something unsafe about meeting a guy this way.

Oh, come on, she told herself. *What kind of threat could Mitch be?* She had just started trying to imagine what he might look like when Abby called to her from the porch steps. "Hey, Nikki! Hey!"

Nikki grinned at Abby, who had Gallie by the collar and was struggling to keep the big dog from bounding in Nikki's direction.

"Adam and I took Gallie down to Rosie's Grill with us and got some French fries," Abby said. "Did you know Gallie really likes fries with ketchup? Hey, what'd you think of Shannon, Nikki? Wasn't she *awesome?* Did you like her?"

Nikki swallowed hard, trying to decide which question she could answer honestly. "No, I didn't know Gallie likes his fries with ketchup."

She walked across the grass to the steps and leaned over to rub the dog's silky ears. "Why don't I take him back home for you now?" she asked, hoping to get away before Jeff's sister said any more about Shannon.

"Sure. Thanks. Hey, Nikki? Jeff was kind of looking for you, about half an hour ago."

"Oh yeah?" Nikki couldn't help feeling a little lift at Abby's words. If Jeff was looking for her . . .

"Yeah." Abby grinned, a dreamy look in her eyes which Nikki found distinctly annoying. "You know how love is. When Shannon had to leave, he just couldn't let her go. He decided to go spend the rest of the day with her family. He wanted to tell you good-bye, I guess."

Right, Nikki thought, remembering that she and Jeff had talked about jogging together later that evening. *He was probably trying to weasel out of it so he could go be with Shannon.*

The blue clapboard house was silent when Nikki closed the kitchen door behind her. She stood still, listening for a moment, but only the steady hum of the refrigerator filled the silence.

"Hey! Is anybody home?" she called at last.

"Nikki? We're all out here on the porch."

Nikki closed her eyes. She had avoided this as long as she could. Taking a deep breath, she straightened her shoulders and walked toward the screen door.

Her mother and Aunt Marta sat in the wicker rockers, their backs to the screen and Lake Michigan beyond. Gram and Grandpa sat close together on the porch swing, but moved apart to make room for Nikki. Gram patted the flowered swing cushion between them.

Nikki sat reluctantly, noting her mother's red eyes and the sniffs from Gram, who put an arm around her granddaughter and hugged her tightly. Aunt Marta, who tended more to action than to tears, was busy tucking straggling strands of gray-blond hair back up off her neck, though they fell again as fast as she let go of them. After a few minutes, she pulled out the clip and started all over, working till her hair was gathered into its usual precarious arrangement at the back of her head as she spoke.

"I'll say it *again—one* of us needs to go *talk* to David. *I* certainly will!" She punctuated each sentence with a sharp nod of her head, making the ends of her hair tremble. "He can't just walk out on you and Nikki like this, Rachel. Whatever happened to the idea of facing your problems and fixing them, instead of just running away from them all? As though that's going to solve anything!" she added in derision.

So it wasn't just a bad dream, Nikki thought. *Dad's really gone.* She'd known it, of course, but hearing other people talk about it made it feel real to her, somehow. She'd been able to hold it all at arm's length while she'd talked with Keesha, while she'd e-mailed back and forth with Mitch. But now there could be no more pretending. "David needs to grow up and quit believing that running off with some other woman will just erase all his problems!" Marta continued. "What an infantile way to think."

Nikki watched her aunt in amazement. *I've never seen this side of her before. She's usually the cool-headed one who figures everything out rationally and then acts. But she sure doesn't know Dad very well if she thinks she could make him face his problems.*

Nikki had witnessed too many arguments between her parents over the years, heard too many doors slam as the "resolution" to every fight, to believe her father would change now. *Mom must be thinking the same thing*, Nikki thought, watching Rachel raise her eyebrows and look sidelong at Marta.

Grandpa leaned forward and rested his elbows on his thighs, hands folded between his knees. "Talking to David is necessary, Marta, I agree. But I think attitude is more important here than anything else."

"You're absolutely right. His attitude stinks!"

There was no answer from Grandpa, and Marta faltered. After a few seconds of silence, she asked, "You're not talking about David's attitude, are you?"

"We won't get very far, just bludgeoning him with anger."

"But I *am* angry," Marta said flatly.

He looked up and smiled. "I had a suspicion that was the case." But Marta did not smile in return as he went on. "We're all angry, honey. David's doing a terrible thing. But our anger will just push him farther away."

"So we don't confront him at all?" Marta shot back. "We just let him go do his thing and blow his family to bits?"

"I didn't say that," Grandpa replied. "I'm saying that first we need to take care of our own hearts, and do some serious praying. No matter who speaks to David, until *God* confronts him, there won't be any real change."

Rachel sprang to her feet. "Oh, give me a break. For once in your life, try to realize that prayer isn't the answer to everything, Dad." She crossed her arms in front of her and turned to stare out over the lake. "You always expect God to come charging in like some knight on a white horse and put all the pieces back together the way they were."

Nikki cringed to see the pain in her grandfather's eyes. But his voice was still gentle when he replied. "I suppose God doesn't do that very often, Rachel. But that doesn't mean He doesn't work in other ways. I don't think you'd want your marriage put back together exactly the way it was anyway, would you?

"But if you were to turn *toward* God, instead of keeping your back to Him," Grandpa continued, "you would find that He can do all kinds of wonderful things you'd never even think of."

"And in the meantime," added the always-practical Gram, "you can stay here with us as long as you want."

Rachel's mouth curved up on one side, her face a study in exasperation. "You know, it's not as though I can just drop my whole life at home and take a vacation. I have classes to teach, commitments to meet—"

Nikki closed her eyes and groaned. As usual, Rachel was impossible to please, asking for help on the one hand and pushing it away with the other.

Gram remained unruffled. "I know, Rachel. You have too much on your mind just now to figure everything out. I understand."

A year ago, Nikki thought, she would have considered her grandmother's words about understanding totally out of place. Gram and Grandpa's life together had always looked so stable, so peaceful. What could they possibly know about a heartbreak like this? But the experiences of the last year—with Gram's life-threatening stroke and what Nikki had discovered they'd faced together before they even got married—gave credence to the older woman's words.

Now Gram, once as feisty as Aunt Marta and plain-spoken almost to a fault, was reaching out to Rachel with a new gentleness. Nikki had not realized until now just how much the stroke and long months of convalescence had changed her grandmother.

"You know we'll be praying that—" Gram said, but Rachel cut in.

"Prayers won't do any good here, don't you understand that?" Rachel clapped her coffee cup down on the glass-topped table. "God—if there really is a God—would certainly not be interested in my marriage. Not after I've ignored him for the last 25 years. Anyway, I doubt even God could change a man as stubborn and hard-headed as David Sheridan."

Her voice was a curious mixture of anger and anguish, Nikki thought, wishing uneasily she were somewhere else, anywhere but here, seeing this.

Grandpa leaned back, looking weary. "God *is* concerned about your marriage, Rachel. And every other detail of your life, no matter where you've been for the past 25 years. But, like I said before, you'd have to turn toward Him—not away."

Rachel's back stiffened. *Here we go*, Nikki thought. *Things are going to get really ugly now.*

Instead, relief came in the click of quick footsteps around the side of the house. A loud voice blared as Arleta made her way up the porch steps.

"SO HERE'S WHERE YOU ALL ARE! I KNOCKED AND KNOCKED AT THE FRONT DOOR AND DIDN'T GET THE SLIGHTEST BIT OF NOTICE, EVEN FROM GALLIE."

Arleta looked around at the five people already on the small porch, smiled, and held out a green Tupperware® container. "I KNEW YOU'D BE NEEDING EXTRA FOR SUPPER, WHAT WITH BOTH GIRLS HOME, CAROLE. SO I MADE AN EXTRA BATCH OF MY HEAVENLY HASH." She started to release the dish into Gram's hands, then thought better of it. "WELL, YOU KNOW IT HAS TO GO RIGHT IN THE FRIDGE, WITH ALL THAT FRUIT AND WHIPPED CREAM IN IT, AND I DON'T WANT TO MAKE YOU GET UP, SO I'LL JUST GO PUT IT AWAY FOR YOU."

She threaded her way among the five pairs of feet on the porch floor and disappeared into the kitchen, talking the whole time. Her voice dipped to almost normal volume as she opened the refrigerator door and bent to look inside. They could hear the scrape of jars and pitchers and bottles being rearranged on the metal shelves; then the refrigerator door shut and Arleta's volume was back to its usual near-painful level.

Nikki shook her head. *She's probably the only person in the entire world who wouldn't catch on to the fact that something* very big *is going on here, right under her nose.*

Arleta reappeared in the kitchen doorway. "NIKKI, I TYPED UP AN ANNOUNCEMENT FOR THE PAPER—FOR THE CHRISTIAN WOMENS' OUTREACH TEA WE TALKED ABOUT LAST NIGHT. I HAVE TO RUN RIGHT NOW, BUT I WANTED YOU TO SEE THIS BEFORE I SENT IT IN."

Arleta passed Nikki a folded sheet of paper, kissed the air beside Carole's cheek, and gave "the girls"—Rachel and Aunt Marta—a quick pat and a smile. "I'VE GOT TO RUN. THE LIBRARY BOARD MEETING STARTS IN FIVE MINUTES." She turned at the door, her face hopeful. "SOME OF US ARE WATCHING *GONE WITH THE WIND* AT MY HOUSE LATER THIS EVENING, IF YOU'D LIKE TO COME."

Grandpa smiled. "I think we'll pass this time, Arleta, but thank you."

The screen door snapped shut. Arleta was gone, but her appearance had broken the tension. Aunt Marta rocked forward and stood to her feet; Grandpa followed. Even Gallie peeked out from behind Gram's flowered house shoes, his brown eyes searching the porch anxiously as if to make certain the source of the noise was gone.

Gram got up and put one arm around Rachel's waist. "Did you bring enough clothes to stay with us until your classes start, at least?"

Rachel hesitated, then spoke so softly Nikki could barely hear. "Actually, Mom, my car trunk is full of luggage. I was so upset, I just threw everything into suitcases and got out of Ohio as fast as I could. I guess I wasn't really thinking coherently."

Gram's arm tightened around Rachel in a quick hug. "Well, one thing I'm still good at is unpacking. Would you mind if I help you?"

It wasn't till everyone else had left the porch that Nikki unfolded the paper Arleta had handed her. When she did, the first line stopped her dead.

"Local Teen Nicole Sheridan Tells How She Got Through Her Personal Crisis," Arleta had typed. The article mentioned other women who would tell their stories also, but Nikki barely scanned that part. Her face burned, just seeing her name in print this way. She could never stand up and talk to people about the most personal, most painful part of her life the way Arleta was asking her to.

Nikki crumpled the paper into a ball and tossed it into the kitchen trash. *Leave it to Arleta to ask for the moon! No way will I tell people all this private stuff. Not even for Gram's best friend.*

$$\infty$$

Nikki spent the late afternoon helping her mother settle into the bedroom across from Gram and Grandpa's, the room that had once been Rachel's own when she was growing up. Gram and Aunt Marta helped too, trying to lighten the mood, but Rachel's anger and hopelessness settled over everything like a dark cloud.

For Nikki, the worst moment came when she and her mother were left alone in the bedroom. Rachel stood still and silent in front of the dresser. She gazed into the mirror, but Nikki knew from the expression on her face that she was not seeing her own reflection. She was looking instead at something deep inside, something far beyond Nikki's ability to see.

She's forgotten I'm even here, Nikki thought.

Nikki watched as slowly, deliberately, Rachel drew her diamond engagement ring and the wide, gold wedding band off the ring finger of her left hand. She held them in her palm and stared at them for several seconds, then opened the top dresser drawer and laid them carefully in a miniature heart-shaped crystal dish.

A cold feeling of finality wrapped itself around Nikki's heart at the *clink* of gold against glass. She turned and slipped quietly from the room.

Six

AT DINNERTIME, FOOD SEEMED the last thing on their minds. Aunt Marta called out for a large pepperoni pizza, but most of it ended up sitting on the kitchen counter, little pools of reddish grease congealing around each circle of meat.

Rachel disappeared upstairs to her room with a headache. Marta and Gram started washing and cutting up salad greens for tomorrow's dinner.

Nikki peeled and sliced two cucumbers, her back turned toward the open kitchen door which looked out on the driveway her grandparents shared with the Allens. She was determined not to keep checking to see if Jeff's red Bronco was back yet. Keeping herself from listening for the sound of wheels crunching over the gravel was another matter, however, and no matter how she tried not to, she found herself picturing Shannon and Jeff together. She knew she needed to get her mind on something else as soon as possible.

Scraping the last of the cucumber peels into the disposal, she wandered out of the kitchen and down the hall toward Grandpa's study. She found him seated in front of the desk, his computer screen dark. Nikki scanned the desktop and noted his Bible, open in front of him.

When he saw her, he pushed back his desk chair and got to his feet. He said only one word, and his voice was unsteady on even

51

that. "Nikki?" He put his arms around her and hugged her tightly. For a moment, there was no need to say anything.

"Would you like to take Gallie for a walk with me on the beach?" he asked after a while. "We haven't really talked about all this."

Nikki was reluctant to even think about her parents, let alone talk about them. "Well, the twins took him for a walk this afternoon . . ."

Grandpa laughed. "Were you worried he might turn us down?" He whistled and then hollered, "Gallie! How about a walk?" The big dog came racing down the hall at breakneck speed, nearly losing his footing rounding the corner of the study doorway. "See what I mean?"

The sand was still summer-hot on Nikki's bare feet. But there was a different feel to the early September air, some faint hint of change on the way.

"You can tell it's time for school again," Nikki told her grandfather as they strolled side by side. "Funny how things can feel so different when everything still looks the same."

"Your senior year! That's pretty big stuff, Nik. Excited?"

Nikki put both her shoes in one hand and leaned down to unleash Gallie with the other. "I was." She straightened up and fixed her gaze on the horizon. "I thought this was going to be such a great year, after getting the pregnancy over with and getting the baby settled in a good home. And with Gram doing so much better after the stroke. Then Mother came and spilled her news."

"There's probably nothing harder than seeing your parents break up," he answered quietly.

Nikki gathered the slender leash into folds and stuffed it into the pocket of her shorts. "Grandpa, I don't even know exactly why this whole thing is hitting me so hard. Our family wasn't great, like the Allens. Mother and Dad never even got along much. So why . . . why does it feel like I'm losing something so—I don't know—so *valuable*?"

Grandpa walked quietly for several steps. Only the cry of the gulls and the gentle lapping of water against the sand filled the silence. " 'Every divorce is the death of a small civilization.' I can't recall who said that, but he or she was right. Your family, good or bad, is your whole world when you're young. And even when you're older, those ties are still there."

Nikki squinted up at the sky. "But I thought with all that happened last year, with Mother and Dad basically walking out on me . . . and me living here with you and Gram . . . I'd made a real break with them. Until Mother told me the news, that is. Then, well, I guess I always hoped . . ."

Her voice broke off as Gallie, who had circled around behind them, now pushed between them in a mad dash at the flock of gulls which had landed on the sand ahead. "Yuk!" Nikki said, brushing away wet sand that the dog's fur had smeared on her leg.

They watched and laughed together as Gallie rocketed directly at the gulls, sending them flapping away in a panic. "He'll never grow up, will he?" Nikki asked.

" 'Fraid not. Ever since we first brought him down here as a pup, he decided his mission was to clear this beach. And to keep it that way at all times," he added in a clipped, martial voice, and they both laughed again.

Nikki stopped, watching Gallie dwindle to a small, golden brown dot far up the thin strip of sand.

"What do you think will happen?" she asked.

Grandpa whistled tunelessly through his teeth for a moment, considering. "With your parents? Well, it's way too early to tell, Nikki. Sometimes people separate and then get back together. As for your mother, I think that depends on which way she turns."

"What do you mean?"

"You probably heard me tell her this when we were out on the porch, though I'm not sure *she* heard me. The most important decision is whether to turn toward God or away from Him."

Nikki's thoughts swept back over the past year—finding out she was pregnant, choosing a home for Evan, and all the rest. "I turned away at first, didn't I? Last winter, when I got so angry about giving up Evan?"

Grandpa nodded. "I think so. It took you a while to work through the shock of it, and the anger. People need time to struggle through that before they can stop shoving God away with both hands—and turn toward Him."

"Mother doesn't even believe in God, she says."

Grandpa peered into the distance, almost as if searching for the future. "Maybe that will change before this is all over," he said softly. "For now, let's give your mother a lot of space, and a lot of love. And don't give up praying for her for a minute."

Gallie barreled toward them, growing larger by the second, a stick of driftwood in his mouth. He broke his run right in front of them and sat down hard in the sand, looking up at them with pleading eyes.

Grandpa laughed as he pulled the stick from the retriever's mouth. "You took care of all those pesky birds, so now you need a little swim, huh?" He tossed the stick as far as he could into the water; Gallie plunged in after it, his golden head held high over the little waves.

They stood side by side, watching, and Nikki finally voiced what was bothering her. "Even though I'm a Christian now, I'm not sure what you mean—to turn toward God. I guess I need to pray and read the Bible and all that. But the stuff I've read doesn't seem to help much. Not in a situation like this, I mean."

She looked down at her bare feet and dug her toes into the wet sand. "And sometimes I don't even know how to pray. Like for my Dad, for instance."

Grandpa put his arm around her and squeezed her shoulder gently. "You know, I don't think there's a better place to look than the Psalms when you're in trouble. Have you spent any time there yet?"

Nikki shook her head. "Aunt Marta got me started reading John, in the New Testament."

"Well, there's nothing wrong with that. But when things get really tough, you'll find good company in the Psalms—the company of other people, especially David, who went through the same things as you and wrote about it very honestly. All their pain and joy and fear and anger—"

"Anger? In the Bible?"

Grandpa laughed. "You bet! More anger than most of us will ever admit to, even though it's there. We try to pretend we're not angry, but David had a much more honest response—he spilled it all out to God and let Him handle it."

Nikki looked skeptical.

"Why hold it in, Nik? Why pretend it isn't there? It isn't like God doesn't know what you're feeling, you know. Anyway, many people find such terrific company in the Psalms that they read some every day. I've been doing it myself for more years than you've been alive. There are enough psalms to read five every day of the month, though I wouldn't push myself to finish all five if you want to stop and spend time in just one. I like to read Psalm 1 on the first day of the month, then add 30 and read Psalm 31, then add 30 and read Psalm 61—you get the idea. On the second day of the month, I start with Psalm 2 and follow the same process. It's a good way to keep your place."

Gallie returned to shore, holding his treasure high above the water, and trotted proudly back to beg for more. Nikki tossed the stick this time and watched the dripping dog plunge happily into the water again.

Grandpa wasn't finished with the subject of Bible reading, though. "Psalms can help you with prayer, too, Nikki. There are lots of times I don't have a clue how to pray, so I just pray through whole psalms for someone, turning each psalm into a prayer, or sometimes just a few verses."

Nikki glanced up at her grandfather. "Were you praying like that for me? Last year, when I was having such a hard time?"

"Who says I ever quit?"

When they got back to the house, Nikki wasn't sure what to do with the rest of her evening. With Keesha off meeting this Steve from the Internet, and Carly away at the clinic, Rosendale felt deserted. She absolutely refused to let herself think any more about Jeff and Shannon. She polished her nails, both fingers and toes, and cleaned out her makeup, then got the bright idea of organizing her school clothes. At least it would keep her mind off everything else. She spent the next two hours laying out clothes on her bed, planning what shirts and sweaters went with which jeans and skirts, trying to get ready for the opening of school, which was now only three days away.

Once everything was out of the closet and stacked on her bed in neat piles, Nikki stood back to survey the scene. "I really should have bought some more jeans," she told herself, resting her hands on her hips. "Black ones."

If I'd been really smart, I'd have saved all that money I spent buying clothes to impress Jeff. It didn't even work. I could have bought four pairs of jeans for that money—

The phone rang, interrupting her work, and Nikki's first thought was that Jeff was finally home. She grabbed the phone off the small table in the upstairs hall, calling, "I've got it!" before she remembered that she was supposed to be upset with him.

The voice on the line, though not Jeff's, was painfully familiar.

"Nicole? Is that you?"

Nikki swallowed hard. "Dad?"

"Hey there, how are you doing?" His voice was too bright, too cheerful. *Too fake*, Nikki thought.

"I'm—okay. I guess."

"Haven't talked to you in a long time."

"Yeah. Since Aunt Marta and Carly and I stopped there on our way to Virginia. Uh, did you want to talk to Mother?"

"Oh, I don't think that's a very good idea," he said hastily. "I just thought I'd call and see how you are, Nikki."

All at once something seemed to burst inside her, and she couldn't stand any more small talk. "Dad, why'd you do it? *Why?* Why'd you leave?"

"Well, now, Nicole. I really just called to talk about you. Sometimes it isn't—appropriate—to discuss personal details with children. I think what happened between your mother and me falls into that category."

"I'm not a *child!* And I think that's a major cop-out! I know things weren't great with you and Mother, but why couldn't you just get help? Why couldn't you get counseling? Why did you have to run off with some other woman?"

Nikki could hear her voice rising, turning shrill. She took the phone into her bedroom, shut the door behind her, and leaned against it.

David cleared his throat, then hesitated. In the brief silence on the other end of the line, Nikki heard voices, laughing voices. Suddenly one of them shouted clearly, "Get off the phone! Come on! You're gonna miss the first pitch!"

"Dad?" Nikki asked. "Who's there with you?"

He cleared his throat again. "Well, you know about Celeste, apparently. I suppose your mother told you all about the situation, though I certainly wish she had let me do that myself."

"Don't worry about what anybody told me. *You* tell me what's going on." *And try to tell the truth for once.*

"Celeste has two children, Nikki. A boy, Michael, who's 12, and a 10-year-old girl. Her name is Madeline."

Something twisted inside Nikki's chest. She had never considered—never once—that this woman would have children. The voice called again in the background, and though his words were muffled with his hand over the receiver, she could hear her father. "Maddy, hold on, sweetheart. I'll be right there."

There was a quality in his voice she couldn't name—a gentleness that swept her back to when she was little, back to the days when he still played with her, before his law practice had begun to consume him. A clear picture of David Sheridan sprang into her mind, of his olive complexion and dark, wavy hair. He was smiling at a little girl Nikki had never met, the way he'd stopped smiling at Nikki years ago.

Nikki felt a wave of jealousy wash over her. Her fingers tightened on the phone until her knuckles ached.

Suddenly she remembered her mother's words, the ones spoken

on the porch last night: *He met her last year, right after we found out you were pregnant.*

Nikki's pulse raced as she fought to stop her mind from completing the thought—but she lost. *Maybe this whole thing is my fault. He was so ashamed of me. If I hadn't gotten pregnant, if I hadn't decided against the abortion, none of this would be happening. Now it's like he's got another daughter, one he can be proud of—*

Nikki felt her stomach lurch. Before she realized what she was doing, she hit the TALK button and disconnected.

She stood there holding the silent phone for several minutes. She stared at the clothes on the bed without seeing any of them, and a loneliness like nothing she'd ever known wrapped itself around her.

"Nikki. Nikki!" It was Gram's voice, calling from downstairs, that brought her back to the present.

Nikki looked down at the phone in her hand. The last thing she wanted was for David Sheridan to call back. She hit the TALK button again, then put the phone under her pillow so no one could hear the busy signal. Finally she opened her bedroom door and walked to the head of the stairs.

"Yes, Gram?"

"Who was that on the phone, honey?"

Nikki hadn't lied in a long time. It was something she'd been careful to avoid since becoming a Christian. But her heart was so numb that she didn't feel a single qualm when she answered, "Just a telemarketer, Gram," and returned to her room.

She grabbed one of the pink-striped throw pillows and settled onto the window seat, staring across the blue water of Lake Michigan.

A new kind of pain was spreading through her chest. Until now, she'd felt bad for her mother; Dad had left *Rachel* for another woman.

But now Nikki felt abandoned as well. She hugged the pillow hard. *He left me, too. For somebody else's kids.*

She stared at the lake until the sky went gray and the water turned a matching shade. Her thoughts wandered, touching places she really didn't want to go, yet couldn't seem to avoid.

He never watched a game with me in his life. Did he watch games all the time with Madeline? *"Maddy," not Madeline. Funny, I used to think that name was cute.*

There was a boy, too. Michael. How did her dad feel about having a boy around? Had he always secretly wanted a boy? *You could've had a grandson—you could have been part of* Evan's *life!*

Did he used to look at me and wish I were a boy? Is that another way I disappointed him?

She shifted on the window seat, leaning her forehead against the window. This was her fault. She felt sure of that now. For the first time in months she thought back to the night when she'd been with T.J., when she'd gotten pregnant.

In my worst nightmares I never could have dreamed up all the bad that came from that night. A shiver of guilt ran through her, and she wanted desperately to reach out to someone, something.

She looked across the room at her Bible that lay on the bedside table. She stood up to get it, then stopped.

Why? What good will reading the Bible do?

I don't want to hear all about how God is a Father. If this is what being a father means, God can keep it for all I care.

She turned and swept the clothes into a pile at the foot of the bed. Then she threw herself face down onto the empty space, pulled a pillow over her head, and wept.

❧ *Seven* ❧

WHEN NIKKI WOKE THE NEXT MORNING and found she'd slept in her clothes, she felt dirty and bedraggled, which did nothing to help her mood. Sometime during the night, the clothes she'd pushed into a pile on the foot of the bed had fallen in a huge jumble on the floor, and that didn't help her mood much, either. Nor did the fact that she'd overslept and had to tell her grandparents and Aunt Marta to go on to church without her, and she'd follow as soon as she could.

And when Arleta cornered her just as she rushed, 15 minutes late, into the church foyer, Nikki thought she'd scream. The Scripture reading was just starting, and Nikki could hear snatches of it over the PA system, in between the words Arleta was, thankfully, doing her best to whisper, for once.

"Our text this morning is from Ephesians chapter four, beginning with verse 22. 'You were taught, with regard to your former way of life, to put off your old self . . .'" the pastor read.

"I've been waiting and waiting, hoping I'd get to talk to you," Arleta said. Nikki looked down at the tiny woman and wondered if she'd ever actually seen anyone wear a hat with a bright red stuffed cardinal on top before.

"Really," Nikki answered, trying not to stare, impatient to slip inside the sanctuary before the whole congregation saw how late she was.

" 'And to put on the new self, created to be like God . . .' " the pastor's voice went on.

"You *have* made up your mind to give your testimony at the tea, haven't you, Nikki?"

Nikki closed her eyes, trying frantically to come up with an excuse. After all that had happened yesterday, there was nothing she wanted to do less.

"Nikki, I have to know *today*. I've got to get the article to the *Rosendale Roster* by nine o'clock tomorrow morning. We really need you. Those girls who will come need to hear your story, so they won't make the same mistakes."

Nikki's thoughts whirled, hunting for excuses. *I'll tell her . . . I'll tell her . . .*

She smiled to herself. *That's it! I'll tell her Keesha and I have something planned that day and I can't possibly speak at her tea.*

Nikki opened her mouth to answer, but just then the pastor's voice boomed over the PA system: " 'Therefore each of you must put off falsehood and speak truthfully to his neighbor. . . .' "

Nikki sighed and shut her mouth. This was impossible. There was no way to get out of it. Through the open doors of the auditorium, Nikki could see Gram looking over her shoulder, studying the crowd behind her and Grandpa to see where their now-outrageously-late granddaughter was.

"I just need to know!" Arleta demanded, her voice starting to edge above the far reaches of a whisper. Nikki had to hush her before she reverted to her normal volume.

"Okay, okay, Arleta. I'll do it. Just, please, don't expect too much. I've never spoken in front of a lot of people before."

Arleta's face lit up. She gave Nikki's arm a little squeeze, then managed to keep her voice down. "Oh, you'll be great, sweetie. I just know it. I have to go to Arnold's—you know my son, the police officer—for dinner today, but I'll come by in the evening so we can talk about what you're going to say. Thank you so much, my dear."

"This ends the reading of the Scripture," the pastor's voice intoned as Arleta walked away.

Nikki gave up and headed for the pew where the Allens sat next to her grandparents and Marta, with the sinking feeling she had just been cornered into a complete and total disaster.

Nikki tried to concentrate on the sermon, but it was a lost cause. Every time she forced her attention back to the pastor, his image faded out and was replaced with a mental picture of herself, standing red-faced before a roomful of teen girls and women. She saw herself babbling, stammering, trying to explain how she'd made the decision to place Evan for adoption, how she'd said no to the abortion, how she'd gotten pregnant in the first place—

She shuddered, then hoped no one had noticed. *You've really done it this time, Nik*, she thought. *This is going to be the most embarrassing experience of your life.*

When they arrived home from church Nikki opened the kitchen door, anticipating the warm, meaty smell of Gram's usual Sunday roast and potatoes. Instead, she came face-to-face with Rachel, who had declined to attend church with them, and who met them now with red and swollen eyes.

"Your *father* called, Nicole," she said accusingly. "Thanks to you, I had to talk to him. He says he's very anxious to talk to you as soon as you can call. Apparently you hung up on him last night. Was that the 'telemarketer' that called, by any chance?"

Nikki stood in the middle of the kitchen, facing her mother and aunt and grandparents, without a word to say. She thought the crunching noise of a car pulling into the gravel drive outside may have been the sweetest sound she'd ever heard, second only to Keesha's voice, calling as she bounded up the kitchen steps to knock on the screened door. "Yo, Nik! You won't believe this. I got a sitter, I got the car, and have I got great news for you—"

Keesha surveyed the family through the screen door and stopped dead in the act of putting her knuckles to the wooden doorframe. "Don't tell me. I came at a bad time."

Nikki moved toward her rapidly. "Oh, no. You came at a *good* time—a very good time." She opened the screen door and nudged

Keesha toward the driveway. "Let's get out of here," she murmured under her breath.

"Keesha and I have to talk," she said quickly to the adults in the kitchen. "We need to make the most of this chance, you know? Keesha doesn't get much time away from Serena, and she hardly ever gets to use the car. Don't wait lunch for me—we'll grab something." The door slammed behind them and Nikki hustled Keesha toward the car.

"You wouldn't want to tell me what that was all about, I suppose," Keesha said.

"We'll talk once we get out of here, okay?"

By the time they were a block away from the blue clapboard house, though, Keesha's interest in explanations had all but disappeared as she bubbled over with her own news. "Family stuff, huh?" she said. "Well, listen, I don't know what it was all about back there, but I had to come and tell you about last night. You would not believe Steve, Nikki. He is *so* hot! There is definitely a future in this!"

"Good time, huh?" Nikki asked.

" *'Good time'*? That doesn't even come *close*, girl. Steve is like, the single best thing that's ever happened in my entire life!"

In her excitement, Keesha had trouble keeping her attention on the road. Nikki found herself unable to pry her eyes off the paved strip ahead, as if willing Keesha's car to stay in its lane.

"You cannot believe how gorgeous he is, Nik! Arms like *this*—" she took her hands off the wheel long enough to curve her fingers around an imaginary bicep of incredible proportions. "And his shoulders!" Keesha kissed the air in front of her. "I absolutely love a guy with *shoulders*, you know? And hot. Did I mention hot? He is so totally, totally hot!"

The more Keesha talked, the faster the words poured out. "*And*, he held the door for me, Nicole. Do you know that no guy in my entire life has ever held a car door for me? But Steve did! He took me to Angelino's, that really expensive place that looks out over Lake Michigan, over on the other side of Howellsville. And he bought me *lobster!* I've never even *tasted* lobster before! But best of all, he brought me *flowers*. *Roses*, Nik, *roses!* Nobody's ever brought me roses."

Keesha would go on for hours this way, Nikki knew. She watched the white lines on the pavement disappear beneath the front of the car and tried not to think how jealous she was. Eventually, though, curiosity got the better of her. "So, when Steve was here, did he, like, say anything about Mitch?" She tried to sound as though it didn't matter to her one way or the other, but Keesha saw through her immediately.

"I knew it! You *are* interested! I knew it!" Keesha was so excited she nearly squealed. The car veered just over the white lines, then back. Nikki's eyes began to ache from staring at the road so hard.

"He talked a *lot* about Mitch," Keesha said. "They've been best friends for years, since eighth grade or so." Keesha blared the horn at a pickup turning left in front of them.

"Keesha, what are you honking for? That guy had plenty of time—"

But Keesha talked on without a break. "And you should've heard what Mitch is saying about *you.*"

Nikki grinned, pleased in spite of herself. "Oh, come on. What could he say about me? We only typed back and forth for a little while."

"Yeah, well, apparently you made a big hit with this guy. A gigantic hit, if you know what I mean! He really wants to take you out, Nik."

Nikki shook her head. "I'm not going out with some guy I met on the Internet, Keesha. I already told you that."

"But why not?"

"Because putting yourself in that kind of situation is *dumb*, okay?"

Keesha sniffed. "Oh, thanks. So now I'm dumb!"

Nikki tried to backtrack hurriedly. "I didn't say *you* were dumb, Keesha—"

"Oh, yeah? *I* went out with a guy I met on the Internet, so I guess that makes me a real jerk, right? Well, let me tell you something, Nikki. While you sat home alone last night, eating your heart out

over Jeff and his new woman, I had the best evening of my entire
life!"

Keesha's voice grew softer, but didn't lose its intensity. "You
could have, too, Nikki. Steve says Mitch is a great guitarist—the two
of you could have talked about music, or any of the other stuff he's
into. Mitch sounds like just what you need to take your mind off a
certain guy who double-timed you. So now, you tell me, Nikki.
Who's the 'dumb' one here?"

It was nearly dinnertime when Keesha dropped her off at home.
Nikki knew she shouldn't have stayed out so long without an explanation, but going home meant facing an angry Rachel, and
maybe even another phone call from her father.

Rachel, who was seated at the kitchen table with a glass of iced
tea, looked up when Nikki entered. "Did you get back to your father
yet?"

Nikki felt her face burn as she recalled her lie about the phone
call. "How could I get back to him?" Nikki asked. "I haven't even
been here to call him, in case you haven't noticed, Mother!"

She saw hurt flash in Rachel's eyes, but there was no time to
apologize. A short rap on the door sounded behind her—and Arleta
let herself in.

I don't believe this, Nikki thought. *We can't even have a family fight
in privacy.*

"I'M SO GLAD I CAUGHT YOU AT HOME," Arleta began in
her usual loud tone, settling herself in a wooden chair across the
table from Rachel. "I KNOW GIRLS YOUR AGE ARE AWFULLY
BUSY THESE DAYS, SO WHEN I KNEW I WAS GOING TO BE
LATE, I WAS AFRAID I'D MISS YOU. BUT ARNOLD JUST IN-
SISTED I STAY LONGER AND LONGER. HOW'S THAT NICE
JEFF ALLEN DOING, BY THE WAY? SUCH A GENTLEMAN,
THAT YOUNG MAN."

Nikki stared at her in amazement. Not only was Arleta's timing
unbelievable, but she had an uncanny ability to zero in on the worst
possible subjects as well.

Rachel poured another glass of iced tea and handed it to Arleta, who looked coyly at Nikki. "DON'T WANT TO TALK ABOUT HIM, HMMM? WELL, THAT'S ALL RIGHT. YOU DON'T HAVE TO SAY A THING. I UNDERSTAND HOW THINGS ARE."

No, you don't! You don't have a clue! Nikki thought about the blond and lovely Shannon and wished she could scream, but knew she never would. At least not at Arleta who, for all her annoying ways of showing it, loved Gram and all Gram's family deeply and faithfully. Besides, there was no chance to scream, even if she would have, because Arleta talked on and on, endlessly and loudly.

"WELL, LET'S GET DOWN TO BUSINESS HERE. LIKE I TOLD YOU BEFORE, NIKKI, WHAT WE NEED AT THE TEA IS A STORY FROM SOMEONE YOUNG LIKE YOU. WE HAVE TWO OTHER LADIES—ONE MY AGE AND ONE YOUR MOTHER'S AGE." She looked at Rachel and smiled. "BUT FOR THE TEENS, WE NEED YOU. I THOUGHT YOU MIGHT WANT TO START BY EXPLAINING HOW . . . WELL, YOU KNOW . . . HOW YOU GOT INTO YOUR . . . PREDICAMENT . . . LAST YEAR."

Arleta hurried on, her wrinkled cheeks flushed slightly pink. "THEN YOU CAN EXPLAIN ABOUT HOW YOU DECIDED TO NOT HAVE THE ABOR—" She broke off, glancing uncomfortably at Rachel. "HOW YOU DECIDED TO GO AHEAD AND CARRY THE BABY TO TERM. AND I'D LIKE YOU TO TELL ABOUT HOW YOU BECAME A CHRISTIAN THROUGH ALL OF IT."

Rachel stopped drinking, mid-sip. She looked first at Arleta, then at Nikki. Her eyebrows went high for a second; then her face went back to its usual impassive expression.

"WHAT WE'RE TRYING TO TELL THE GIRLS IS HOW GOD CAN USE ANY SITUATION, NO MATTER HOW DIFFICULT IT LOOKS, TO BRING US TO HIMSELF."

Nikki squirmed. *Sure,* she thought. *God did that. But look what happened to my family when He did it!*

Rachel cleared her throat softly, then pushed back her chair and left the room.

"Something tells me my mother doesn't agree with you," Nikki murmured.

Arleta tilted her head to one side. "WHAT WAS THAT, DEAR?"

Nikki shook her head. "Nothing." She sighed. "It's not important."

❦ *Eight* ❦

DINNER WAS A SUBDUED AFFAIR that evening, though Gram and Aunt Marta had gone to obvious lengths to cheer Rachel. Marta concocted her best shrimp scampi and Gram contributed lemon meringue pie, both high on Rachel's list of favorite foods. But she hardly seemed to notice.

When the dishes were cleared, Jeff called. "Hey, Nikki," he said. "Want to walk with me to Rosie's Grill for an ice cream?"

What's the matter? Nikki thought. *Can't find Shannon to go with you?* But she didn't say it. Glancing at the tense faces around the dining room table, she realized her only other option was to sit here in the gloom.

"I'll be right out," she said into the phone.

Walking to Rosie's with Jeff was such a normal part of their usual summer routine that Nikki had to work hard to keep reminding herself that everything had changed, now that Shannon was on the scene. For the entire walk, Jeff kept telling stories about freshman orientation at the university that made her nearly double over with laughter. Then she would remember how he'd betrayed her and she'd stop laughing and try to figure out how to bring up the subject of Shannon. It wasn't like she could just blurt out, "Look, buddy, I'm jealous of this gorgeous new friend of yours." Nothing would make her admit those feelings to Jeff. She was growing more and more exasperated that he could laugh and make her laugh when they ought to be discussing what had happened at brunch yesterday.

Each time she stopped laughing, Jeff would look at her questioningly, then launch into another tale that made her laugh before she could help it. *It's like he doesn't have a clue*, she thought, exasperated. *In fact, if I didn't know better, I could swear he doesn't even know he hurt me.*

Finally, as they walked home side by side licking their cones, Jeff stopped and stared at her. Nikki stopped, too, and glanced up at him. "What?" she demanded.

"Why don't you just give with what's bothering you, already? Like I've told you a million times, I've known you so long I can read your mind, lady."

Nikki sighed. Guys could be so—what was it Marta always called them?—*obtuse.*

Swallowing a mouthful of cookie dough ice cream, she started walking again. "Fine, then. Since you can read my mind, you tell me what's bothering me."

"Oh, come on, Nik—"

She shook her head as they reached the back steps of her grandparents' house. "No. If you don't know, I'm not telling you."

He knows, she thought. *He has to know. And I'm going to make him admit it.*

Even as she said it, Nikki knew how childishly she was behaving. *I'll talk to him about Shannon*, she decided, *as soon as we get inside*.

The kitchen was empty, the counters clean and shining, but the sweet smell of lemon meringue pie still hung in the air. Jeff sniffed, then grinned. "Your aunt's been at it again, huh?" It was a well-known fact that whenever Marta came to visit, she did much of her relaxing in the kitchen.

"Up to my elbows in flour and sugar—that's the best way I know to get my mind off work," she always joked. Cooking was a welcome break from her hectic schedule of teaching at Indiana University and the conferences she did around the country throughout the year. And this year, added to all the rest, was the pressure of the book on folk music she was finishing.

Nikki's grandfather always commented how lucky it was for them that Marta chose this way to relax. "In fact, I think you need to relax a lot more, honey," he often told her. "I've heard that making chocolate cake is the most relaxing of all, actually. Doesn't that sound relaxing to you, Carole? Nikki?" he'd poll them, straight-faced, and Gram would roll her eyes at him and try not to laugh.

This time, though, Nikki shook her head no. "Nope. Aunt Marta just did her shrimp scampi—"

Jeff groaned. "And I *missed* it?"

"—and Gram did the pie," Nikki finished. She pulled open the refrigerator door and ran down the drink choices. Jeff picked Pepsi, then got glasses and ice for them and poured. Brown foam bubbled down around the ice cubes in his glass as he asked, "Your grandma's making a super recovery, you know that? I mean, think back to where she was this time last year. And now she's baking pies and doing housework."

Nikki sipped soda from her glass, nodding. "I would never have believed she could get this far."

Jeff took a long drink, then set his glass on the counter. Nikki had just opened her mouth to bring up the whole subject of Shannon, when a burst of laughter from the front of the house stopped her.

Jeff frowned in Nikki's direction. "Did that sound like Abby to you?"

The first laugh was followed by another, slightly lower and definitely Adam's. Jeff and Nikki tracked the laughter to the study, where they stopped just outside the door to listen.

There was a giggle from Abby, then a snort from Adam.

"Oh, man!" Adam said. "Are you gonna swallow that kind of junk? He's coming on to you."

They could hear Abby sniff. "Like you know! I think he's kind of sweet."

Jeff pushed the study door open wide. Abby and Adam startled at the sight of him. "So," Jeff began, trying to sound casual, "what are you two doing in here?"

"Uh . . . Grandpa was helping us find some stuff on the Internet," Adam said.

"Oh, yeah? I don't see any Grandpa around."

"He said we could stay," Abby said defensively.

"He just went upstairs to say goodnight to Gram," Adam added.

"And we weren't doing anything wrong!"

"So don't pull your big brother act on us!" Adam finished.

"Hey, chill out for a minute, you two. All I did was ask a question." Jeff's voice was mild as he looked over their shoulders at the computer monitor. "Meeting some new friends here, huh?"

Abby clicked the BACK arrow quickly and the screen reverted to a home page. Nikki had just enough time to catch the words "Romance Connection" before Abby clicked again. A cursor blinked beside an empty prompt box, asking what search engine the user preferred.

"We were just messing around, Jeff," Abby continued. "Honest. You don't need to say anything to Mom and Dad."

Nikki leaned against the side of the desk. "If you aren't doing anything wrong, why don't you want him to tell your mom and dad?"

Jeff answered, looking at the twins. "We have this agreement at our house that we're all accountable to each other for whatever Internet sites we visit. Dad says it's way too easy to hit sites that are bad for you if nobody else knows what you're doing. That's why they put our computer in the family room where all the traffic is. We're supposed to let each other know where we went after we've been on the Internet."

"We were just meeting some cool people, that's all. We weren't doing anything wrong!" Abby insisted, her braces glinting in the light from the green-shaded desk lamp.

"Glad to hear it," Jeff said. "But what do you say we let Nik's grandpa in on our family policy when he comes back? I'm assuming you didn't quite get around to telling him yet."

Adam hung his head. "Not yet."

Nikki could hear footsteps coming down the stairs. "Sounds like you're about to get the chance," Jeff said.

Grandpa walked through the doorway of the study and stopped in surprise at the sight of Jeff and Nikki. "I didn't know you two were back. Have you seen my computer prodigies here?"

He nodded toward the twins, who avoided his eyes as they scooted from behind the desk to make room for him. "They've caught on to this Internet business a lot faster than an old guy like me. I bet they could teach me a thing or two about navigating the Web."

"I bet you're right there," Jeff muttered, so only Nikki could hear.

Grandpa stopped halfway into his chair. "Have I missed something?" He settled down on the seat and waited. The twins stammered quick good-byes and dashed out the door.

Grandpa turned to Jeff, his eyebrows raised in question.

Jeff stuck his hands in the pockets of his khaki shorts and hesitated a second before plunging in. "Remember the other night, how Keesha warned you about not giving out your password, sir?"

Grandpa nodded. "Sure. She said people could get into my e-mail and research—"

"Well, there's other reasons you probably don't want to let the twins work alone on your computer. I mean, I don't know if you've heard much about all the garbage you can get into, but there's a lot of stuff—" Jeff stopped, obviously uncomfortable.

Grandpa was quick to try to ease his discomfort. "Are you talking about all the pornography, Jeff? I know about that. That's why I signed up for a blocking service, so that sort of thing isn't available." His white brows gathered together and a look of alarm flickered in his eyes. "Abby and Adam didn't stumble into anything like—"

"No," Jeff reassured him. "They didn't get into any pornography."

Grandpa sighed his relief, then frowned again. "Then what was the problem?"

Nikki perched on the corner of his desk. "There's other stuff on the Internet that can cause trouble, Grandpa. Abby and Adam were looking at some Romance Connection thing, and Abby was talking to one of the guys there. From what Adam said, he was coming on to her, but she just thought he was 'cool.' " After her online chat with Mitch, she couldn't help feeling hypocritical as she spoke.

And how is that so different from what you did with Mitch, Nikki? she thought suddenly. Frowning, she brushed the idea away.

Grandpa passed a hand across his forehead, his face troubled. "I only left for 10 minutes, just long enough to go upstairs and kiss Carole goodnight and pray with her. It takes me so long to get around on the Web, I had no idea they could get in trouble that quickly."

Jeff smiled and shrugged. "I wouldn't worry about it. I don't think there was any harm done this time. You might want to talk to Dad about what he and Mom did with our computer so this kind of stuff wouldn't happen. Dad's told me about a couple situations where people got into real trouble, meeting people who weren't what they claimed to be on the Internet." He looked at his watch. "I guess I don't need to go into all that. But that's what made my parents be so strict with our computer." He started toward the door. "I think I better go check on the twins."

Nikki walked with him to the kitchen door. Jeff turned to her apologetically. "We never did finish talking, I know, but we'll have all day tomorrow, right? I'll call you later if I can."

Nikki nodded, wanting desperately to ask if he was bringing Shannon to the annual Nobles-Allen Labor Day picnic, but couldn't bring herself to do so. *What is it about even the thought of that girl,* Nikki wondered as she watched Jeff's tall back across the graveled drive, *that turns me speechless with Jeff?* Her mind gave the answer almost as soon as she'd thought the question. *Fear. Fear that she's taking your place with him.* Jeff disappeared into the Allens' house and Nikki stood staring after him blankly, realizing that was the reason she became tongue-tied, thinking of Shannon. It would be easier not to know, at least for a few more days, if what she feared was really happening.

⌒⌒

As she walked back through the kitchen, Nikki saw Arleta's iced tea glass still sitting on the table and remembered with a sinking feeling in her stomach that she now had a whole speech to develop. A speech she couldn't even imagine giving. *And in just a week!* she thought. *I don't have any idea how to do this.* Nikki climbed the stairs slowly, and once in her room, lifted her journal from the drawer of the bedside table, then curled up in her usual spot on the window seat. Gallie ambled in after her, dropping heavily onto the carpet and regarding her with friendly, brown eyes.

"Sometimes I think you have it made, dog. No worries about dating, no speeches to give." She sighed. "And I don't think there's any such thing as dog divorce. You don't know how lucky you are, do you, Gallie?"

At the sound of his name, the dog thumped his tail wildly and started to get to his feet. "Down, boy!" Nikki ordered. "You just rest. I have work to do here."

Maybe if I read through last summer's journal entries, she thought, *I'll get some ideas.* It was all here, wasn't it? Finding out she was pregnant . . . Gram having the stroke . . . her parents trying to force her to have an abortion, and telling her not to come home until she did . . .

She tried to read, but couldn't concentrate. Along with the painful memories of last summer, all the new turmoil of the last three days kept getting in the way.

It's too much, she thought, setting her journal down. *You get through one crisis, and there's another. I've got nothing to tell those women. They want a success story, and I'm a failure.*

"This is a time for prayer," she remembered Grandpa telling her when Gram lay in the hospital last summer, unable to respond in any way. He'd said nearly the same thing to Rachel on the porch, about the issue of David leaving.

Nikki thought back to those terrible nights when she lay in bed, asking God to heal Gram. Asking God to help her know what to do about the baby. Now Gram was well on the way to recovering, and Evan was settled with his adoptive parents, Jim and Marilyn Shiveley. There were still times when her heart—and her arms— ached for him. Times when she heard another baby cry unexpectedly at the mall, or turned the corner in the grocery store and saw a baby in one of the grocery carts that looked to be close to Evan's age, and her heart seemed to stop. But she could see him every six months, under the terms of the adoption, and the Shiveleys sent pictures and descriptions of him faithfully each month. She was learning how to love him from afar.

You did answer my prayers, Lord, she thought. *Not exactly the way I wanted, and certainly not as fast as I wanted, but You definitely answered.* She thought again about what Grandpa had said about reading through the Psalms and reached for her Bible.

It was September 5, so she started with the fifth Psalm.

"Give ear to my words, O Lord,
    consider my sighing.
Listen to my cry for help,
My King and my God,
For to you I pray."

Nikki stopped, staring at the words in amazement. *That's exactly what I would have said if I'd thought of it. David is asking for the same thing I am—help. Lord, I want You to listen to my words about my mother and dad. You know what my dad is doing, and it's really hurting me. And it's killing my mother.* Aunt Marta had encouraged her to start reading the Bible shortly after Nikki had first become a Christian last winter, and she had tried hard to do it regularly. But somehow, the words had never come to life this way before.

"In the morning, O Lord, you hear my voice;
    in the morning I lay my requests before you
    and wait in expectation."

She stopped again, surprised this time by David's confidence. "He just took it for granted that You heard what he asked You, and he *expected* You to answer, Lord!"

Gallie thumped his tail against the carpet at the sound of her voice and started to rise.

"Gallie, just relax, would you? I'm not talking to you!"

Nikki read the verses one more time, then again. Something was going on inside her she couldn't define, a kind of feeling that she was connecting in a new way to God. For the first time, she under-stood that what she was reading in the Bible was written to *her*. *"There are lots of times I don't have a clue how to pray, so I just pray through whole psalms for someone, turning each psalm into a prayer, or sometimes just a few verses,"* Grandpa had said.

Slowly, hesitantly, she tried it. It was confusing at first, because she read a verse, then closed her eyes out of habit and prayed it, then opened them again to read the next verse. Finally, she decided the Lord could hear her just fine with her eyes open.

"In the morning, Lord—and in the evening too, I guess, since it's evening right now—You hear my voice." There was something strengthening about affirming it out loud. "In the morning—and evening—I lay my requests before You and wait. In expectation. I'm asking You to take care of what's going on with my mother and father. Change their hearts. Let them listen to You. Let them become Christians. And—if You wouldn't mind—I could really use some help figuring out how to make up this speech for Arleta's tea."

There was such a strong certainty that God was right there with her as she finished that she actually found herself glancing around the room. She grinned at what she'd done, but still there was ex-hilaration inside her. She could just come to God and tell Him what she needed and wanted and He would do it. David had.

But you're certainly no David.

The thought was so definite that Nikki felt the excitement inside her start to fizzle. Hadn't she heard in one of the sermons at church or somewhere that David was a "man after God's own heart"? No one could say that about *her*, for sure.

It was late when the phone rang. Nikki ran to the phone table in the hall, knowing Gram needed her sleep. She took the phone back to her room, then hesitated. *What if this is Dad calling back?*

The phone rang again in her hand, and she pushed the TALK button. To her relief, she heard Keesha's voice on the other end of the line.

"Nikki! I just got an e-mail from Mitch, and he wants your e-mail address. He wants to take you out this weekend!"

Nikki started to protest, but Keesha talked right over her. "Listen to me, Nikki. He is really interested in you. He wrote and was asking all kinds of stuff. Now stop being so stubborn and go e-mail him, would you? I didn't give him your grandpa's address 'cause I knew you'd kill me, but here's his."

Keesha read off Mitch's e-mail address. Nikki couldn't help being a little interested, but she protested even more strongly to cover it up. "Keesha, why's he want to take *me* out? If he's so hot, don't tell me he can't find anybody else to go out with, not in a city big as Detroit."

"Nikki, did anybody ever tell you that you have a suspicious mind?"

Nikki turned and rested the side of her head against the cool glass of the window. "Yeah, so maybe I do."

Keesha laughed. "Oh, Nik, come on! Do you still think these guys are killers? I spent the whole evening with Steve on Saturday, remember? Don't you think I could tell if he was *dangerous*? Or into drugs, or weird or something? Just e-mail Mitch back and give him a chance."

"Keesha, can you hold on for a sec? I have another call."

Nikki switched to the other line and was surprised to hear Jeff's voice. She got off her call with Keesha and came back to him, feeling both delight and apprehension. She wanted to talk to him, sure. She just didn't want to hear all about the wonderful Shannon.

"Hey," he said, "I felt kind of bad about our walk to Rosie's. I wanted to talk about more serious stuff tonight, but I got goofing off and then got distracted with finding the twins in the study and all. I know you have a lot of stuff going on that we should have talked about. I just thought maybe it'd do you good to laugh a little." He waited for a second, and as soon as she made a "hmm" sound, he went on. "So how are things going? With your parents and all?"

"I'm not sure how to answer that, Jeff. Nothing else has happened." She wished she could tell him about the phone call from her father, but it was still too fresh, too hurtful. "Nothing much, anyway."

"Well, Shannon and I looked for you yesterday. We were going to ask you to ride back to Shannon's with us. She really liked you, you know."

Nikki mumbled something, but Jeff went on anyway.

"So, what'd you think, Nikki?" he asked.

"About what?" she stalled.

"You know about Shannon. Did you like her? Do you think the two of you could be friends?"

No. To both your questions, she thought. But aloud, she asked, "Why do you care what I think, Jeff?" She hated the whiny tone she heard in her voice, but Jeff didn't seem to notice.

"Because you and I go back 15, 16 years, and I trust your judgment about other girls. Listen, I don't know if this'll make sense to you, but it was great to find another Christian right in the middle of the U of M orientation. Sort of an answer to prayer, you know?"

Great. How am I supposed to argue with an 'answer to prayer'? Her heart began to ache more and more. *He used to talk this way about me,* she thought, remembering what Carly used to report to her. *Until I stupidly told him I wanted to just be "friends."*

Once Jeff hung up, after assuring her they could talk more about it tomorrow at the picnic—the Nobles and Allens had been sharing a Labor Day picnic as the last event of the summer for as long as she could remember—Nikki sat silently on the window seat, trying not to feel the sadness and depression that overwhelmed her. *So maybe you're right, Keesha. Maybe you do have to be open to meeting new people and all that. Maybe now I'm ready to take that risk.*

Nikki replaced the phone on the hall table and went downstairs to Grandpa's empty study. She knew her grandfather wouldn't mind if she used the e-mail, though she doubted he'd be pleased at who she was e-mailing.

Hi, Mitch,

Keesha told me you'd been asking questions about me. I guess that makes it my turn, right? To ask about you, I mean.

She sat for a moment, then typed some more.

What do you do for fun? She looked at the sentence, thinking how dumb it sounded, then deleted it.

Do you play any sports? That sounded a little better, but not much.

This was going to take longer than she'd thought.

By the time she finished, she'd written a page and a half. She read it through one more time, then clicked SEND.

When Nikki dragged herself out of the study, it was after midnight. The house was silent. She started for the stairs, then noticed that someone had left a light on in the kitchen. She walked down the hall to turn it off, knowing how Gram hated to waste electricity.

To her surprise, the kitchen wasn't empty.

Rachel sat motionless at the table, her hands cupped around a black mug, the string and tag of a teabag hanging over its edge. Nikki hesitated in the kitchen doorway, then stepped closer.

"Mother?"

There was no answer, not even a hint that she had heard. Nikki spoke louder.

"Mother!"

Rachel swung around to stare at Nikki. For a second or two Rachel's eyes didn't seem to focus. Finally she set her cup on the table and began to pull the teabag up and down through the water absently by its tag. "Hello, Nikki."

"Do you mind if I sit down?" Nikki asked. She wanted to go to her own room, to bed, anywhere that Rachel, with all her sorrow and pain, was *not*. But how could she run away and just leave her own mother alone at a time like this?

Rachel sat up straighter in her chair, cleared her throat, and seemed to come back to the present. When she spoke, her words jolted Nikki. "I've been sitting here wondering something, Nicole. Do you have a picture of your baby? Of Evan?" She turned the black mug in her hands and stared at the purple nasturtiums on the side. "He's my grandson, and I've never even seen him."

Nikki sank into one of the wooden chairs across from her mother, openmouthed. Of all the things Nikki might have thought could happen, this was definitely not one of them.

Rachel went on, staring intently at her mug as though it held some important key to deciphering the mess her family was in. "I told myself last year that I had to go along with what your father wanted. When we tried to force you to have the abortion, I mean. I think I sensed, even back then, that he wanted out of this marriage, and I—I felt I had to do anything I could to keep him here." She set the mug down with a bump and looked across the table at Nikki. "So I betrayed you, Nicole, and betrayed my grandson. And lost your father anyway. I don't even know the words to say how sorry I am."

Nikki was still staring at her mother, speechless. *She's acting like a real mother, not stiff and aloof and totally unemotional.* It was the oddest thing she'd ever seen, Nikki thought. Rachel looked exactly like she always did—perfectly permed, wheat-colored hair, porcelain skin with every minute flaw covered at great cost in time and money. But inside those expertly made-up eyes, there was a hint of something different, something softer, more vulnerable, and Nikki wanted to reach out and grab it, hold on to it, before the old, hard Rachel returned.

"You want to see Evan?" she finally was able to ask. "You really do?"

Rachel nodded and her eyes filled with tears.

"Hang on," Nikki said, pushing her chair back from the table. "I have a whole album of him upstairs, in my room. You won't go anywhere, right?"

She ran to the base of the stairs and started to pound up them, then remembered that her grandparents and aunt were sleeping. It wasn't till she tiptoed inside her bedroom that her eyes fell on the window seat, where her Bible and journal still lay, open, and she remembered the prayer she'd said earlier that evening.

"Change their hearts," she had asked for both her mother and her father. *"Let them listen to You."* She didn't know for sure if that was going on with Rachel, but *something* was happening, something very different. She breathed a quick *Thank You!* and headed back downstairs with the album of Evan clutched against her chest.

Rachel and Nikki pored over the album together for the next half hour, scrutinizing each picture for details. Rachel pointed at one of Evan sitting in his swing. "You know what? He looks exactly like you did at that age, Nikki. *Exactly.*"

She looked up and her eyes searched Nikki's. "You are allowed to visit him every six months, isn't that right?"

Nikki nodded.

"Do you think—would you mind—if I went with you to see him next time?"

It was after 1:30 A.M. by the time Nikki went back to her room, but she was so excited that she began working on her testimony for Arleta's tea and was up till 3:00. If God could change Rachel that fast, He could do anything. Anything at all. Even make Jeff stop liking Shannon and start liking Nikki again. Even bring her dad back!

❦ *Nine* ❦

NIKKI OPENED ONE EYE slowly, groggily. Sunshine poured in through the windows, and she knew it must be late morning.

Ugh. My last day of freedom. A lot of things about school were okay, she had to admit. But she wasn't crazy about the getting up and getting ready by 7:30 part.

She forced her other eye open, then sat up suddenly. *Jeff'll be at the picnic today.*

The Allen-Nobles Labor Day picnic was a long-standing tradition. Jeff would have to return to Ann Arbor tomorrow, but at least they had this one day. And after what had happened with Rachel last night, who knew what could happen with Jeff?

Maybe he'd already seen that Shannon wasn't for him. Maybe he was as excited about seeing Nikki as she was about seeing him. Again, the thought rushed through her mind that had deflated her enthusiasm earlier: *You're no David, Nikki.* This time, it was followed by an even more disturbing thought. *Get real. Why would God want to answer your prayers? Especially after the trouble your actions have caused in your family.*

But look what happened last night! With my mother, she began to argue, then stopped and pushed back the bedspread and jumped out of bed. This was no time for theological debates with herself. It was the last time she'd have a whole day with Jeff for who knew how long.

She threw open the closet door and wondered for an instant where all her clothes had disappeared to—then remembered with dismay that they were still on the floor at the foot of the bed. She sighed, then squared her shoulders, determined not to despair at the sight of the jumbled pile of jeans and sweaters and shirts on the carpet.

From the pile she plucked a pair of white denim shorts and a sleeveless, orange, knit V-neck top that looked especially good with her dark, curly hair—and that Jeff had once said looked terrific on her.

I'll get to the other clothes later, she told herself, *after the picnic*. The important thing now was to get ready. And to look her best.

There seemed to be an unspoken agreement to make this last day of summer the best it could possibly be. No one mentioned David Sheridan; everyone seemed eager to help Rachel have a good time. Marlene Allen and Rachel, who had known each other since their children were babies, stretched out side by side on the shabby chaise lounge chairs Grandpa had lugged upstairs from the basement and set up in the side yard between the houses.

Grandpa and Dr. Allen stood side by side, arms folded across their chests, scrutinizing their houses and yards, comparing notes on what needed to be nailed down and taken in and cleaned up before another bitter Lake Michigan winter blew in. Aunt Marta and Gram carried huge bowls of potato salad and Jell-O® past them on their way to the picnic table and overheard their conversation. Gram stopped and looked at Grandpa with a teasing expression. "Roger, you've been telling us for the last 10 years that you're going to have that porch roof repaired. You don't expect us to believe it again this year, do you?"

The men raised their eyebrows at each other, then went on with their discussion, purposely ignoring Gram.

Marta stopped at Nikki's side. "Hey, kiddo, do I know you? Let's try to get some time to talk today before I have to leave. I feel like I've hardly even seen you since I got here." She started to walk away, then turned back. "By the way, I had a *very* interesting conversation with your mother over breakfast. Something's very different about her the last day or so."

Just then Gram called for help with the table. "Talk to you later," Marta said, and hurried away.

Nikki looked forward to the chance to talk to Marta, but for the moment, there was a more pressing question. *Where's Jeff?*

She couldn't bring herself to be obvious enough to ask about him. *What if he changed his mind and decided to go spend the day with Shannon's family? What if he left early to go back to U of M?*

The thought made her angry enough that for a moment she hoped he wouldn't even show up. But just for a moment.

I've got to talk to him before he goes back. If she could force herself to bring up the subject, she'd find out that Shannon was just a friend, just a good potential study partner, just—

Oh, stop it, you idiot! she told herself. *Stop believing in fairy tales.*

Still, she caught herself looking around the yard and scanning the shore far below. Then, seeing Jeff jogging up the steps from the beach, she sighed her relief. He'd been for a run, that was all.

When he reached the yard, Jeff came straight toward her. Nikki tried to look absorbed in talking to Gallie.

"Hey! Just the person I wanted to see," Jeff said, wiping his sweaty forehead with the bottom of his T-shirt.

I doubt that. She couldn't forget how Jeff had looked at Shannon just two days ago. But instead of saying anything, she just glanced up at him, acting slightly surprised. "Why?"

"What d'you mean, 'why?' " He frowned, looking uncomfortable. "Labor Day's always our special day to just hang out, or go out on the boat or whatever. It's kinda strange without Carly, though."

His blue eyes looked empty for a moment, and Nikki's feelings did an about-face, touched by how deeply he missed his sister.

She reached out and squeezed his arm gently, trying to reassure him. "Carly will be fine, Jeff. They know what to do for her at the clinic. And she really wants to get better. When I talked with her in

Virginia, she was totally committed to beating this eating disorder thing."

Jeff's eyes searched hers for a long minute, as though hanging on to her strength. Then the corners of his mouth curved upward. "Thanks, Nik. I guess I really needed to hear you say that."

Having Jeff need *her* was a new experience. It seemed to Nikki that, for the last year, she'd done all the needing. She basked in the warmth of his comment for a moment, then Gram called her to come help set more food on the picnic table. The next few hours were busy, with eating steaming grilled chicken and cold potato salad, playing volleyball, then sprawling on the shady lawn to relax and talk.

By late afternoon, however, it was obvious that Abby and Adam could stand only so much relaxing. Soon they were begging for one last ride on *Another Line*, the trim blue-and-white boat christened by their doctor father. Carl Allen always got a huge laugh out of having his secretary tell people he was on *Another Line* when they called his office.

"This is our last chance, Daddy!" Abby pleaded, her braces glistening. "We won't get another boat ride till next summer. Please!"

Carl stretched with a groan in the chaise lounge where he lay. "Oh, Abby, a boat ride's a lot of work for an old guy like me. I won't get another chance to lie around like this till next summer, either. Besides," he opened one eye and looked at Nikki's grandfather, "didn't we have a date with one of those gorgeous bass when it cools off a little, Roger? Down off the end of the pier?"

Grandpa nodded, straightfaced. "Two or three of them, I thought I heard you say."

"Grandpa and I have been trying to get out fishing all summer, Abby, honey. Why don't you and Adam come with us? You guys used to beg to go fishing."

Abby rolled her eyes. "Oh, Dad, I'm not into all that gross stuff anymore. We want to take a ride down to Saugatuck and walk around and shop and—"

"And get fudge at that place where they make it while you

watch," Adam put in, closing his eyes in blissful anticipation. "Double chocolate rocky road, the kind with the nuts and marshmallows and—"

"Adam, you just ate *four* pieces of chicken," Marta reminded him.

Adam looked at her innocently. "I know," he said as though making an excuse, "but we ran out."

While Marta laughed, Jeff pulled himself up off the grass and stretched his arms high above his head. "Come on, I'll take you guys in the boat. Nik'll come too, I bet."

Good old dependable Nik, Nikki thought. *You can always count on Nik when Shannon's not around.* Even so, she wouldn't have missed going. When else would she get to talk to Jeff face to face? And there was a strong feeling of relief in the air, as though the adults were glad they'd finally have a chance to talk alone about all that was going on with Rachel and David.

Lake Michigan was exactly right for a boatride today, Nikki thought an hour later as Jeff slowed *Another Line* to dock in one of the few empty spaces left at the Saugatuck harbor. The water was calm and sparkling blue, and there was just enough light breeze to riffle her hair and cool the brilliant sunshine that beat down across their shoulders.

Saugatuck was crowded with boats from across Lake Michigan, vacationers taking one last break from Chicago before summer officially ended. Jeff and Nikki and the twins walked across the weathered gray wood of the boardwalk toward the little downtown area. Even from two blocks away, the thick, sweet smell of fudge hung in the air. Adam drew in a long, appreciative breath, then started toward his favorite shop in a race-walk.

"Come on, you guys. I don't want it to close before we get there!"

Nikki and Jeff trailed the twins past gift shops and art galleries, coming to a breathless stop at the open doors of Adam's favorite store. White-smocked workers poured heavy, slow-moving batches of fudge onto huge marbletopped tables. People crowded to the railing, watching and inhaling deep breaths as the sweet mixtures were rolled out into thick slabs. On the other side of the store, a long line snaked toward the ice cream counter, while those just served walked away with huge waffle cones topped with rounded scoops of green and pink and white, studded thickly with bright red cherries and brown nuts or chunks of chocolate.

Abby was in the ice cream line almost before anyone could blink, and Adam stood transfixed, his eyes glued onto the latest batch of double chocolate rocky road fudge being concocted.

"Looks like we'll be here a while," Jeff said, bending down a little so Nikki could hear his words in the crowded store. "You want something?"

Nikki grinned up at him. "Not in here. Not after Gram's peach pie and all that potato salad. I think I just want some fresh air before I overdose on the smell." They motioned to the twins to explain where they were going, and stepped outside to wait. As they leaned against the back of one of the green wrought-iron benches that lined the sidewalk, Jeff asked again about her parents.

Nikki deflected his question, knowing that if she began to discuss the situation, the chance of her crying here in public was high. Better just to let it be until they could talk privately, she thought, and Jeff seemed to understand without much explanation.

For the rest of the afternoon and early evening, they combed the shops and galleries, then strolled the boardwalk, inspecting the yachts docked there. As the sun sank lower in the sky, Jeff and Nikki shepherded Abby and Adam back toward *Another Line*, over the twins' loud protests.

"Just knock it off," Jeff finally told them. "I'll catch it from Mom and Dad if I don't get you back in good time. We all have to get up at the crack of dawn tomorrow and get going. I've got to get back to Ann Arbor, and you all have to get the boat put away and pack up the house."

Nikki groaned, thinking of school starting and of how little she'd done to get ready. "I can't believe we're back into the whole school routine tomorrow. It seems like a whole 'nother world."

"You start school *tomorrow?*" Abby said, her eyes wide. "We don't have to start till we're ready this year, 'cuz Mom's home-schooling us."

"Don't rub it in," Nikki told her, "or I'll have to remind you that this is my last year, but you still have six more to go!"

Their ride back was highlighted by the ever-deepening beauty of the sunset. Airy cirrus clouds lined the horizon as they left Saugatuck, and by the time they neared the Rosendale channel, the feathery clouds were edged in brilliant gold and coral. Behind them, a thin sickle moon already gleamed in the gathering dusk.

The evening was reminiscent of the boatride they'd taken to Saugatuck the summer before, only then Carly had been with them. For an instant, Nikki missed her intensely. But her frustration at not being able to talk privately with Jeff overwhelmed even missing Carly.

We've spent the whole day together and never talked about Shannon, she thought. *At this rate, I'll never find out how he really feels about her.* Nikki was determined not to let him leave for Ann Arbor till they had talked—really talked—about what was going on between them.

Jeff cut the motor as they turned into the Rosendale channel. Lights bobbed around them as they glided almost silently past the NO WAKE sign. Laughter from people strolling and fishing on the pier drifted out over the water, and Nikki smelled the smoke of someone's cigarette mixed with the faintly fishy scent of the lake.

Jeff finally maneuvered *Another Line* into position by the dock. "You two get on up to the house now, okay?" he said to the twins. "Tell the grownups we're home safe and sound. But Nikki and I are going to stay down here for a while and talk."

The twins scrambled out of the boat, rocking it back and forth crazily. Nikki grabbed the side to brace herself, and Jeff reached a hand toward her. "Come on up here with me, Nikki."

She waited till the rocking all but stopped, then steadied herself with his strong fingers as she moved carefully to the seat beside him. They were silent for a moment, watching the last faint threads of gold glimmer and fade in the sky. With the final light of sunset gone, stars appeared, then grew brighter. Nikki listened to the water lap gently, rhythmically, against the side of the boat.

"Guess this is it for another summer, huh?" Jeff's voice was quiet, almost sad.

Nikki's heart lifted. *He doesn't want to leave.*

"Aren't you excited?" she asked. "About going back to U of M?" *Say no,* she thought. *Say you want to stay right here—with me.*

Instead, he shifted slightly in his seat and answered, "Oh, absolutely. It's great in Ann Arbor."

Nikki's heart sank.

"It's just not Rosendale, that's all." He laughed at himself. "That was profound, huh? What I mean is, for as long as I can remember, I'd look forward all year to being here in the summer. There's just something about this place—the lake, the dunes, going out in this boat.

"But this year was so different," he continued. "It was kind of like summer never happened. Carly stayed back in Chicago working, most of the time, except when she went on that trip with you and your aunt. And I hardly got to see you at all."

Nikki smiled to herself in the dark. *He missed me,* she thought. *He wants things to be like they were before, I know it!*

"Not that we should always be together," he added hurriedly. "I don't mean that. We have our own lives."

Nikki's heart fell so fast, she felt like the boat when the twins got out, bobbing up and down wildly.

"Anyway, all I'm trying to say is, it's like we've turned some big corner, you know? Or is it just me, going off to college and all? I mean, last year it was still the three of us, you and Carly and me, all in high school. It didn't seem like it would ever really end, no matter what everybody told us. And now—" He broke off and shrugged.

"Now it turns out 'everybody' was right," Nikki finished. "And no, it's not just you, Jeff. I feel it, too. It's weird, the way

Carly's gone, and I'm a senior, and you're—you're . . ." *And now you're with Shannon,* she thought. But aloud she said, "And now you're this big U of M freshman. Basketball star. All that good stuff."

Jeff snorted. "Right. At U of M, I'm more like—a fly on the wall, practically. All the big jocks strut around like they own the campus, and nobody even knows my name. I'm starting to wonder if I'm invisible."

"Not to Shannon, apparently."

Nikki bit her lip as soon as she'd said it, wishing she could snatch the words back. But still she held her breath to hear his reply.

Jeff swung around to face her, but it was too dark to read his expression. "Shannon? I think Shannon's mostly impressed that I can find my way around campus. She's just got this weird kind of— *innocence* about her."

Nikki's thoughts flashed ahead of Jeff's words for an instant, adding *innocent* to her short list of all the things Shannon was *not*.

"On the one hand, Shannon comes across like she's so sophisticated. But on the other, she really needs someone to show her around. See, you're really strong, Nikki, because of what you've been through, but Shannon's not like you," Jeff said.

To Nikki, Jeff's words meant only one thing. *He's talking about me having Evan. When you're pregnant, everybody keeps telling you that the important thing is to forget what you've already done, to go on and do the right thing, that everything will work out. But no one ever forgets. Jeff hasn't forgotten. Shannon's the "innocent" one, and I'm the one that's been around. That's the only reason Arleta wants me to speak—because of what I did.*

All Nikki's hopes for getting back to a normal life seemed to be crumbling around her. No one would ever think she was the same after having a baby, and she'd been a fool to think so. *And my dad. Look what he's into, because of what I did.*

Nikki turned her attention back to Jeff, who was still trying to explain about Shannon.

"See, to me, Shannon is—" But whatever Shannon was, Nikki

didn't find out, even though she'd been waiting all day just for that one bit of information. Instead, Dr. Allen's voice from the dock broke in on their conversation.

"Jeff? Nikki? Is that you two out there? Come see what we caught! This may be the biggest bass anybody's pulled in around here in a long time! For myself, I think we ought to call Guinness and get this thing recorded right away!" Dr. Allen and Grandpa stood side by side on the dock, faint silhouettes in the walkway light, holding a huge fish between them.

Jeff hauled himself up out of his seat and started for the dock immediately. Nikki sagged against the backrest and closed her eyes in frustration.

After an hour of picture taking and measuring the overgrown fish from every angle conceivable, Nikki ended up climbing the stairs to the house alone. Gram and Aunt Marta and Rachel were still in the lounge chairs, talking under the moonlit sky, a citronella candle burning between them to keep away mosquitoes. Nikki was just about to sit down with them and rehearse the whole fish story when Marlene crossed the yard.

"I can't imagine where they are, Carole," she said. "It's not like Jeff and Nikki to keep them out so late—*Nikki!* I didn't see you there in the dark. When did you get back?"

"We've been back for at least an hour, I think," Nikki said.

"So Abby and Adam are down at the dock with their dad?"

Nikki shook her head. "No, Jeff sent them up here as soon as we docked. He knew you didn't want them out real late."

Marlene clamped both hands to her hips. "Where in the world could they be? They're not at our house, that's for sure."

"Did you check ours?" Gram asked. "They're probably in there watching TV or something."

"Why would they be in your house when everybody else is outside?" Marlene stopped herself and held up both hands, laughing. "And would somebody tell me why I keep trying to make their actions make *sense?* Carl says that if we figure out every situation logically, then expect the exact opposite, we'll always know what the twins are going to do next!" She turned and disappeared toward the blue clapboard house, and within a few minutes, Abby and Adam could be seen leaving the Nobles' and heading across the driveway to their own house.

❧ *Ten* ❧

NIKKI WOKE THE NEXT MORNING feeling everything inside her was unsettled. There was sadness, knowing Jeff had left before dawn for Ann Arbor. There was frustration, because their goodbye the night before, interrupted by an overgrown bass, had left her exactly where she was before—in the dark about Shannon. There was also excitement about the first day of school, and a hope that this year, she'd really get to know some of the other girls. Last year, she'd gone to Rosendale High only out of necessity, because her parents wouldn't allow her to come home, pregnant, to Ohio. Her pregnancy had formed a kind of barrier between her and the other students, except Keesha. This year, though, she wanted to be part of things, the way she had been back in Ohio before she ever got pregnant.

Along with her feelings about Jeff and school, there was the hurt and anger about her parents. Aunt Marta had left to get back to Indiana University in time to teach her first class this morning, and Nikki already missed knowing she was there, ready to talk whenever she was needed. Then there was the speech she was supposed to have ready by Sunday afternoon.

Nikki cocked her head and held perfectly still for two seconds, listening, and added another feeling to her already-long list: consternation. What on earth was Arleta doing in the kitchen this early on a Tuesday morning? The kitchen was directly below Nikki's bedroom, and Arleta's voice carried easily through the open windows.

"Ten more minutes," Nikki mumbled into the sheet. "Just give me ten more minutes and I'll be ready to do this."

But as soon as she tried drifting off again, she remembered that she'd intended to start reading Psalms every day, following Grandpa's advice. She'd already missed Monday.

Right this minute, though, she wanted nothing more than a few more minutes of sleep. She struggled with herself, fighting back and forth between what she wanted and what she knew she ought to do, then realized she wasn't getting any rest anyway.

Nikki threw back the covers and reached for her Bible, opening it on the bed beside her. "Do not fret because of evil men . . ."

Nikki read the line again, then once more. *All I'm doing these days is fretting, especially when it comes to Dad.*

She felt a surge of frustration. It seemed kind of unreasonable to tell her not to fret when her father had left the family and moved in with another woman. *I could use some help here, Lord,* she prayed. *It's not like I can just tell my mind to stop thinking about it, You know? What am I supposed to do?*

She read on. The next several verses seemed to give her a kind of answer, even though she wasn't sure she understood them completely.

"Trust in the Lord and do good;
dwell in the land and enjoy safe pasture.
Delight yourself in the Lord
and he will give you the desires of your heart.
Commit your way to the Lord;
trust in him and he will do this:
He will make your righteousness
shine like the dawn,
the justice of your cause like the noonday sun.
Be still before the Lord and wait patiently for him;
do not fret when men succeed in their ways,
when they carry out their wicked schemes.
Refrain from anger and turn from wrath;
do not fret—it leads only to evil."

Nikki stared at the verses for a moment before she read them another time. If she was reading this right, it sounded as though she was supposed to be thinking about God, trusting Him, and getting closer to Him, more than about the trouble. And somehow, He would take care of things. She lay there staring at the ceiling for a minute, trying to make sense of what sounded like a very hands-off approach to her. Then the alarm went off again, and Nikki closed the Bible quickly, making a mental note to talk to Grandpa about the Psalms the first chance she got.

Arleta sat at the kitchen table, drinking coffee with Gram and Marlene and Rachel when Nikki went downstairs.

"I thought you guys were spending the whole day packing to leave," Nikki told Marlene. "And getting the boat put away and all."

"That was the original plan. Then Carl caught his giant fish and now he has fish fever. He and the twins are out on the boat right now—"

"Along with your grandpa—" Gram put in.

"—determined to break their own record. Carl says we can always drive back here on Friday and get the boat put up for the winter." Marlene rolled her eyes dramatically.

Arleta jumped in. "NIKKI, THAT SHIRT IS SUCH A LOVELY COLOR. I REMEMBER THAT LIME SHADE WAS SO POPULAR IN THE SIXTIES, AND HERE IT IS BACK AGAIN. WHY, I THINK YOU'LL MATCH WITH THE PAPERS I BROUGHT FOR YOU."

From the floor Arleta lifted a huge straw tote bag adorned with pink daises. Setting it on her lap, she took out two oversized posters—black marker on fluorescent green paper—and held them toward Nikki.

"What's this?" Nikki asked as she took them.

"POSTERS! FOR THE TEA, OF COURSE."

Nikki stared at the signs, puzzled. "But why did you bring them here?"

"THEY'RE FOR YOU TO PUT UP AT SCHOOL TODAY!" Arleta said in a tone that implied any two-year-old could have figured this one out.

Nikki set the posters on the table and reached for her glass, trying to act nonchalant. "Oh, I don't think I'll have time to do that, Arleta. Sorry." She poured herself some orange juice, avoiding the woman's eyes.

"WELL, WHY NOT, NIKKI? HOW ELSE WILL WE GET THE WORD OUT AT THE HIGH SCHOOL?"

Rent a billboard. Nikki's thoughts whirled out of control for a minute. *Stand in the school parking lot with a megaphone. Make an announcement over the PA system. Drop them on the parking lot from a plane. Just don't ask me to do it! Most of the kids don't even know I'm a Christian yet, and I don't exactly feel like standing up and announcing it.*

"JUST PUT ONE UP ON THE BULLETIN BOARD BY THE OFFICE AND THE BULLETIN BOARD DOWN BY THE GYM—"

Nikki cleared her throat. "I think you have to have permission to do that kind of stuff."

Arleta smiled. "OH, IF THAT'S WHAT'S BOTHERING YOU, WHY DIDN'T YOU SAY SO? IT'S ALL TAKEN CARE OF. I TALKED WITH WANDA, THE SECRETARY IN THE FRONT OFFICE, AND SHE SAID IT'S FINE."

Arleta gathered her things and pushed back from the table. "I'VE GOT TO GET GOING. I HAVE AN APPOINTMENT WITH DR. VANDER ZOWEN IN HOWELLSVILLE IN HALF AN HOUR." She patted Nikki on the back as she passed her chair. "I KNEW YOU'D WANT TO HELP GET THE WORD OUT ABOUT THE TEA, NIKKI. ESPECIALLY SINCE YOUR NAME'S ON THE PROGRAM."

Gram walked to the door with Arleta, the two of them discussing Dr. Vander Zowen's newest idea for treating Arleta's arthritis. Marlene left, saying that even if the rest of her family had taken leave of its senses, she could at least begin packing.

Meanwhile, Rachel glanced down at the lime green flyers, then back up at her daughter.

"You're really going to stand up in front of all these people and tell what happened to you?" she asked, looking puzzled.

Nikki gulped down the last of her orange juice. "Looks like I have to. I told Arleta I would."

"And you're going to put up these posters at school today?" She sounded incredulous.

All at once Nikki found herself posing a question she would never have thought she'd ask. Maybe it was because, for at least a few minutes, they had connected in the kitchen during their late-night talk. Whatever it was, she suddenly heard herself say, "Why don't you come to the tea and hear me?"

Rachel shifted in her chair, obviously uncomfortable. "I don't know if I'll even be here by then. I have to get back to Ohio to teach."

"I thought your classes didn't start till next week," Nikki asked.

Rachel didn't answer.

"Well," Nikki went on, "if you're around it'd be nice to have you there."

The beginning of the school day was a madhouse.

Nikki tried to get there early to put up the posters without drawing attention to herself. Instead, her Mazda ended up in line behind the first two buses of the day. Then, just as she held one fluorescent green poster up to the bulletin board outside the Howellsville High School office, the first crush of students poured into the hall behind her. More buses were unloading by the minute, so she quickly pushed a tack through the poster to the corkboard behind it, rolled the second poster into a tube, and tried to walk away. By then, however, the confusion had started.

The location of senior and junior homerooms had been left off the printed schedule sent to all students during the summer. Nikki quickly found herself surrounded by other upperclassmen, all waiting for an announcement on where they were to go.

Keesha, looking sleek in a simple, white silk tee and black jeans, weighed down with chunky silver jewelry, pushed her way to Nikki's side. Nikki held the fluorescent green tube low, hoping Keesha wouldn't ask about it.

Keesha was still bubbling over about Steve and oblivious to everything else. "We spent a couple hours on the Internet yesterday," she said. "I just feel like I've found—a soulmate, you know,

Nikki?" Keesha stopped, looking slightly abashed, and shifted her backpack to the other shoulder. "We like all the same things, and there's always something to talk about. I could really go for this guy, if you know what I mean. And Mitch told Steve to tell me to tell you—"

The principal's voice came over the PA system, announcing the locations of the senior and junior homerooms. She and Keesha made their way together, in slow motion, toward Room 10, passing the green poster on the bulletin board. Two junior girls who shared a Spanish class with Nikki, Hollis McCaffrey and Noel Jacobs, were studying it; Nikki strained to hear their reaction, but couldn't.

When the girls turned away from the bulletin board, the taller of the two, Hollis, addressed Nikki. "Aren't you the Nikki on this poster, the one who's going to speak?" It was as though Nikki had never made enough of an impression on her to be remembered.

Nikki nodded and smiled. "Um . . . yes," she answered, wondering what might be coming next. Hollis and Noel were known around Rosendale High as intellectual types. They were both National Honor Society members, intense about their studies and everything else they did.

"I don't think I've ever heard you say two words in Spanish class," Noel volunteered, shrugging back the long, black hair that hung over her shoulders in washboard ripples. "What are you going to speak about at this tea?" She scrutinized Nikki, waiting for an answer.

Nikki swallowed. *Help me out, please*, she prayed quickly.

"I'm going to tell about what happened to me last year," Nikki finally replied.

"Oh. Being pregnant, you mean?" Hollis said, sounding bored.

"Why would you want to tell people about *that*?" Noel put in. She glanced at Keesha. "Hey, you were pregnant last year, weren't you? Are you talking, too?"

Keesha shot Nikki a quizzical look. Nikki shook her head slightly, as if to say, *I'll explain later.*

Hollis pulled the tips of her brown hair—barely longer than Keesha's—down around her thin face. You could always tell when she was intense about something, Nikki thought, because she started blinking her heavy-lidded brown eyes rapidly, as though trying to dislodge something stuck in her contacts. "Have all the people who are speaking been pregnant? Is that the deal here, to tell us how not to get pregnant?"

Nikki shook her head as the crowd finally started to move slowly down the hall. "No," she said, struggling to be heard above the din. "I mean, it's not just about that. It's about how God can work in all the messes we make of our lives."

"What?" Hollis asked. "I can't hear you."

Nikki spoke again, this time much more loudly. "It's about how God can help us when we mess up our lives!"

Just as she said the words, a whole group of students turned in at the door of Room 8, cutting not only the size of the crowd but the noise as well. Nikki found she'd been nearly yelling, and a couple dozen kids were staring at her.

Among them was Chad Davies. As soon as their eyes met, she knew she was in for a bad time. Chad had played a big part in her life right after she'd had Evan, and she'd hardly talked to him since.

He hasn't changed, she thought as he pushed through the crowd toward her and Keesha. His nearly-black eyes and eyebrows still struck a startling contrast to his thick, blond hair. With his button-down oxford shirt and pressed jeans, Chad had a way of making the other guys look sloppy just by comparison.

Hollis opened her mouth to begin another question, but Chad broke in. "What's this I see on the poster back there, Nik?" he asked. "You turning into a street preacher on us?"

Nikki pressed her lips together, determined not to respond to his insolent tone. She knew that if she ever let on how much his teasing bothered her, he'd keep at her mercilessly.

What he actually did, though, was even worse. He slipped into a hellfire-and-brimstone routine, sounding like a tent evangelist in a bad movie.

"Ah, my brothers and sisters, flee from the wrath to come!" His arms waved wildly, and most of the kids stopped dead in the hall, preferring entertainment to homeroom, and watched with expectant grins. They knew Chad's routines.

"Come to the altar! Confess your sins to the Rev. Sheridan," he pointed at Nikki, "and be saved! Right here on the spot!" Laughs erupted here and there throughout the crowd, and Nikki wanted nothing more than to crawl under a classroom door and disappear forever.

Hollis, however, surprised her by speaking sharply to Chad. "Come off it, Davies. You can be such a jerk." Then she turned back to Nikki.

"The tea's not going to be *anything* like that, Hollis," Nikki said quickly.

"No?" Hollis asked. "It's just you and these other people, talking? No yelling or carrying on like that idiot was?" She blinked rapidly in Chad's direction.

Nikki shook her head. "Absolutely not. It's just a couple of us talking about how God can take care of us, even when we get into trouble."

She was sorry as soon as she said the words. Chad, following close behind, jumped on them.

"*In trouble?* Well, Nikki ought to know all about getting *in trouble!* Better go hear her, Hollis, cause she's an expert. In fact, I might even have to go hear Nikki talk about that." He waggled his eyebrows suggestively.

Nikki couldn't help remembering some of the last, mocking words he'd said to her that night at the concert, just before his accident, when she wouldn't let him go as far with her as he'd wanted to. "*You know what, Nik? I think you ought to stop pretending to be something you're not. . . . Why do you think I take you out, anyway?*"

Her cheeks burned. She heard the words over and over in her head as the bell rang and everyone pushed even harder to get to homeroom.

∽

Chad sat directly behind her in homeroom and blew off her angry silence. "Hey, I was only teasing out in the hall," he said. "You never could take a joke, could you, *Nicole?*" He reached forward and helped himself to the copy of her schedule that stuck out of her backpack.

"Hey, Nik, look at this. We have trig and government and English together!" Nikki rolled her eyes but didn't reply. "We'll have so much time together, it'll be like the old days. Just like when we were going out, huh?"

Nikki snatched the schedule out of his hands and turned back toward the front of the room, ignoring him.

The day seemed to go downhill from there. Keesha and Nikki had hoped to have more classes together this year, but found out that they shared only P.E. and side-by-side lockers. Keesha spent the entire P.E. period talking about Steve—which did nothing to help Nikki, who had been exerting all her willpower to not think about Jeff.

Jeff, way over on the other side of the state, sharing all his classes and probably all his meals and for all she knew, all his free time—with the perfect Shannon. Make that the perfect, innocent Shannon.

Even Nikki's locker seemed to be in on the plan to create havoc with her first day as a senior. The metal door stuck fast, no matter how many times she jiggled the cold, silver handle or kicked the door. She finally had to go to the office and fill out a request for the maintenance man to take care of it.

And all the time, simultaneously with whatever she was doing, Nikki was aware of another track running in her mind, the constant ache over what was happening to her mother and father. It was almost as though there were two Nikkis now, the one acting out her first day as a senior, the other watching helplessly from the sidelines as her family was torn apart.

Once, while waiting in the cafeteria line, she gave a fleeting thought to the verses she'd read this morning in Psalm 37. But they seemed to have little to do with the activity swirling around her. She wished she knew some way to connect with God right here, in all the craziness.

The day seemed to last forever. *This is not the way I'd envisioned the first day of being a senior, that's for sure,* she thought, as she finally trudged out the double doors and across the parking lot to the Mazda.

But bad as the day had been, nothing prepared Nikki for what she found when she arrived home that afternoon.

Eleven

NIKKI TURNED THE BLUE MAZDA into her grandparents' driveway—and nearly ran into the rear end of her father's sleek, sage-green Chrysler.

She braked sharply, then stepped out hesitantly. *What on earth is my dad doing here?* she wondered.

Her curiosity turned to anger. *How can he even show his face here, after what he's doing?*

And right alongside the anger, there was a tinge of hope.

She hurried to the kitchen door and went inside. "Dad? Dad!"

Gram was at the counter, peeling potatoes. She looked up, and Nikki could see the concern in her eyes. "Gram, where's Dad?" Nikki asked.

"Well, he was in here for a little while, talking with your mother. But they got pretty upset, and David left for a walk. He said he'd be back when you got home from school. He wants to talk to you, honey."

Nikki slid her backpack onto the table and headed back out the door. "I bet he's down on the pier. He always used to walk there." Just as she reached the door, Rachel's voice sounded from the hall doorway.

"And while you're down there with him, you can tell him not

105

to show his face in this house again, as long as he's acting like an idiot!"

"Rachel!" Gram set down the potato and peeler on the counter. "No good will come from putting Nikki in the middle of this. Or from calling David names."

But Rachel was not to be stopped. "Give me one reason why I shouldn't call him names! It's true, isn't it? He is an idiot!"

Nikki flew out the door and across the grass to the edge of the yard. From here she could see the pier and beach spread out below. Sure enough, David was there, walking the pier, his head bent.

Nikki took the steps two at a time at first, then more slowly as she approached the bottom. What could she say to him, anyway? It wasn't a good sign that he and Mother had been arguing.

She hesitated on the bottom step. *If I tell him how much this hurts, how much I want him to come back and get counseling and put our family back together, I know he'll listen. I know he used to care about me, at least when I was little. I know he'll listen to me, if I just say the right things.*

She tried not to think about Maddy, or about the other woman he was seeing. Jogging up the sand, she neared David as he stepped off the pier and back onto the beach.

"Dad!" she called.

David's head snapped up and he waited while she ran toward him. "Oh, Dad!" The words seemed to rush out of her on their own, bright with hope that the situation was about to change. "Dad? I'm so glad to see you."

All that had happened between them in the past year seemed to vanish in the intensity of what she wanted to say to him. She wanted to hug him, but hesitated just long enough to make it impossible. She ended up standing awkwardly, arms at her sides, waiting for him to respond.

His wavy dark-brown hair was a little longer than he normally wore it, and there was something different about the way he held himself that Nikki couldn't quite define. He tossed his cigarette into the sand and ground it out of sight with the toe of his brown leather loafer.

"Come on, let's walk, Nik," he said.

It was easier, she noticed, walking side by side than facing each other. After a few moments her father asked, "So, how have you been? How was your first day back to school?"

Nikki felt a wave of irritation. *How can he even mention stuff like this when our whole family is falling apart?*

She brushed the irritation away, remembering her determination to say the right things. "Dad, I'm sorry I hung up on you the other night. I—I was just so . . . hurt."

David looked uncomfortable, but didn't answer.

"Dad, tell me what's going on. Why'd you do this? I don't understand. I mean, things were the same as always when Aunt Marta and Carly and I visited you and Mother on our way to Virginia. Then, two weeks later, you're gone! How can a person just leave his family and go off with a mistress—"

"You can just stop right there, Nicole," her father ordered.

Nikki looked up, confused. "But what'd I say?"

"Don't you ever call Celeste names again, do you hear me? I will not have you speaking disrespectfully of her, understand? She's going to be my wife, and I simply will not allow you to talk about her this way."

Nikki's lips trembled, and she blinked back tears. "Your wife? You're going to *marry* her?"

Nikki felt as though the sky were crumbling around her. She had assumed that if she said the right things, he would at least agree to give counseling a try, or do something else to put the family back together. Instead, he was talking about plans—permanent plans— to destroy their family forever.

David stopped walking and turned to look at her. His gaze was calm and steady, but Nikki had the impression that he was carefully choreographing that expression, the way she'd seen him do when arguing a case in court. She knew there had to be more going on underneath the surface than he showed. His words, when he spoke, were condescending.

"Nikki. I'm sorry that you're upset, but you're going to have to understand. These things happen. People stop loving each other. Old families end, new families are created. I'm going to start a new family—a stepfamily, Nik. And you're welcome to be part of it."

Nikki shook her head. "You've been lying to us all year, haven't you?" she demanded. "Lying and cheating?"

David sighed and looked away briefly, then back at his daughter. "Nikki, could you be a little more careful with your words, please? I mean, really. *'Mistress'*? And *'lying'*? I don't think we need to insult each other here."

"Then what *should* I call what you're doing?" she cried. She whirled away for a second, then turned back, anger tensing every muscle in her body. "Fine. You want other words, I'll give you other words. How about 'prevaricating'? How about 'committing adultery'? How about just being an absolute, despicable *fake*?"

David's mouth turned up on one side in a mirthless grimace. "Really, did you expect me to be impressed with your vocabulary, Nicole?"

"Yes! Would you like to hear some of the words I know for *'mistress'*? How about—"

You're losing it, she warned herself. But she wanted to go on and on. She wanted to scream about how it felt to be replaced by someone named Maddy.

"*That* will be enough, Nicole! I warned you before."

They stood eyeing one another, hostile, until at last she gave up and turned to stare at the horizon. "Dad, I'm sorry. I said that to hurt you, because you hurt me. But it wasn't right."

She caught a glimpse of his face, shocked more at her apology than at the other things she'd said. To her knowledge, she'd never heard David actually apologize for anything. "I wanted to ask you if, just maybe, you would consider coming back and getting counseling, you and Mother."

He looked at her for a moment, then shook his head slowly and definitely.

"Dad, *please*. Families aren't supposed to end up this way. Parents aren't supposed to just *walk out*. Aren't there some rules about this or something?"

"Nikki. You're too young to understand. I told you, people change. They grow, and sometimes that growing is apart from each other. And then the love's just not there anymore. How can you keep a marriage going without love?"

Nikki stared at him in frustration. "And what happens when you fall out of love with *this* woman?"

But he only looked at her condescendingly.

She looked away, biting her lip. There was something so wrong with what he was saying—totally wrong—but she didn't know how to explain it. She'd never even thought about the whole divorce thing much before. Her parents might not have gotten along very well, but they weren't the kind who just split. At least, she'd never thought so.

She tried again, her voice timid. "What about *me*, Dad? Doesn't what I want count for anything?"

For a second, he hesitated—then launched into another series of sentences that sounded like a canned speech. *The kind he'd use in the courtroom to tell why the jury should acquit his guilty client*, she thought.

"At first, the situation will feel strange to you, Nikki. But people are ... adaptable. You'll get used to it. Eventually, you'll feel at home when you come to visit Celeste and Maddy and Michael and me."

He's like a stranger, Nikki thought. *He shuts out everything except what he wants to hear*. It was no use reasoning with him, trying to explain her pain. His mind had narrowed down, and now his life revolved completely around himself. He couldn't even hear her pain.

Still, she heard herself try one last time. "Dad, please, I don't want our family broken apart this way. I don't want a stepfamily. I don't want to share you with someone else's family. Please, Dad, please."

When he looked at her, his eyes were steady, unmoving. "You'll understand someday, Nikki. When you've grown up, matured a bit."

Then I hope I never grow up! she screamed at him silently. *I hope I never "mature" enough to step on other people just to get what I want.*

It took all the self-control she could dredge up to stand there on the sand staring into his eyes, and not shout the words out loud.

That's what he wants, she sensed somehow. *He wants me to get hyster-ical, lose my cool. Then he can keep on fooling himself, thinking he's superior, wiser, more grown-up.*

Help me reach him, Lord Jesus. I can't do it on my own. Help me! She prayed, then heard herself switch tactics—saying things she hadn't expected to say.

"Dad, I know you don't claim to be a Christian, but have you ever given any thought at all to what the Bible says about what you're doing?"

David arched one dark eyebrow and looked at her. "Okay, my little preacher, what does it say?"

Nikki hesitated, her legs trembling a little. "Well, I don't actually know, not yet. I just think the Bible says you're not supposed to do this."

"That's rather subjective, don't you think?" David murmured.

"Well, it's not like I had time to look up the exact verses," she countered.

David smiled at her, just a tiny smile, but it encouraged her to add the only thing she knew about the subject—something she'd heard in a sermon.

"I just know that somewhere in the Bible, it says God *hates* divorce."

The sudden change in his expression shocked her. It was as though the words had hit him broadside. David's eyes grew dark with anger; his eyebrows bunched together the way they did when-ever he was close to losing control.

The trembling spread from her legs to her midsection. She glanced around her, wishing there was a place to sit down and steady herself. Her father's anger had always reduced her to feeling like a child, and now she stuttered a little as she tried to explain. "Dad, I-I'm just t-telling you what I've heard. In sermons and stuff."

Still he glared, his gaze holding hers in a vise grip she could not break. "I'll look up some of the verses, do some s-studying, and tell you what I find out, okay?"

David held up both hands to stop her. "No, Nicole. *You* listen to *me.* I came here to extend the olive branch, hoping we could all behave like civilized adults about this situation. Instead, I've been called an idiot by your mother, and a liar by you. The woman I love has been referred to as my mistress, and now you've even enlisted *God* on your side."

He dropped his arms and stuffed his hands into the pockets of his chinos. "So if you don't mind, I think I'll spare myself any more slander and name-calling from you. Few things disgust me more than a moralizing bunch of self-righteous *Christians*." He turned and headed for the steps.

"Dad! *Dad!*" Nikki called after him, following for a few steps until he waved one hand behind him as if to shoo her away.

She stopped then, and stood still in the sand, watching her father stride up the steps and skirt the side of the blue clapboard house. Then he was out of sight.

A car door slammed and a motor roared to life, almost simultaneously. She knew he would maneuver the Chrysler around her Mazda and drive over the grass, not even waiting for someone to move the little blue car.

Twelve

NIKKI ARRANGED AND REARRANGED the three meatballs nestled in tomato sauce on top of her spaghetti, but the thought of putting them in her mouth made her feel nauseous. *At this rate, I might actually end up skinny,* she thought.

Rachel, on the other hand, ate steadily, as though accomplishing a distasteful but necessary task. She cut her spaghetti with angry jerks of her knife, and each time she forked a meatball into bite-sized pieces, the silverware cut through the meat to the china with a sharp *clink.*

Only Gram tried to maintain an atmosphere of normalcy. She asked about Nikki's first day back to school. She questioned Grandpa as to how his article on plankton was progressing. She passed the salad for a third time, then stopped with the bowl in mid-air.

"Marlene and the others got off about noon," she said.

No one answered.

"They just couldn't get everything done before they had to leave, so I guess they'll be back up on Friday," Gram said, trying again. "To get the boat into storage and get the house ready for winter. 'Course I don't think they mind the chance to see Jeff again, either."

Nikki looked up from her meatballs. "Jeff's coming back, too?"

"That's what Marlene says," Gram answered, putting the salad bowl into motion again. "It's only three hours for him to drive here, too. He just comes from the other direction now."

Nikki looked doubtfully down at her spaghetti. *Great. We can get the latest Shannon report.*

After that, no one seemed able to think of more conversation.

After dinner, Nikki took her homework to the back porch. It seemed strange to be learning Spanish vocabulary on an evening that still felt so much like summer. She almost expected Jeff and Carly to come around the corner any second, asking if she wanted to walk to the pier.

It took 20 minutes and several tries, but at last she realized she was accomplishing exactly nothing on her Spanish assignment. Nikki closed the book and notebook and set them on the wicker end table, then went inside to the kitchen. Gram was putting the last of the meatballs into a Tupperware® container, and she looked up and smiled as Nikki entered.

"Not a very good night for homework, I suspect," she said, as she opened the refrigerator door and set the plastic container on a shelf.

"That's an understatement," Nikki said. She sat on the edge of the counter, swinging her bare feet back and forth slightly as she watched her grandmother wipe the rim of the sink and the chrome faucet until they shone.

"It's hard to work when there's so much on your mind," Gram said. "I'm awfully sorry about what's happening, honey."

"Yeah," Nikki said quietly. "Thanks." She took an apple from the fruit bowl on the counter beside her and held the stem with one hand while she turned the fruit absently around and around with the other. When the stem finally snapped, she looked up. "Gram? Can I talk to you for a minute?"

Gram nodded as she reached behind her to untie her apron. "Anytime, Nikki, you know that."

Nikki recounted the conversation she'd had that afternoon with David. She groped for words to describe his hardness, his lack of concern for her feelings. "I tried to tell him what I thought you or Grandpa would, but I don't even know if I got it right. I told him I thought it says somewhere in the Bible that God hates divorce, but I don't even know where."

Gram nodded, her lips pressed together. "You got that part right, honey. Just look up Malachi—that's the last book in the Old Testament—chapter two, and read it for yourself. Jesus says a lot about divorce, too, in the New Testament."

"Really? What's He say?"

" 'Don't.' "

Nikki set the apple back down in the fruit bowl, a smile starting to turn up the corners of her mouth. *Now there's a Gram answer,* she thought. Grandpa liked to give long, involved explanations, but Gram knew how to get to the point.

"Okay, so I was on the right track," Nikki said. "But I need to ask you one more thing." Her smile faded. "Dad said that people change, and I know that's true. But he said that sometimes they change so much there's no love there anymore, so you can't keep a marriage going."

Nikki hesitated, then continued. "If that's so, then I don't think I want to get married. I mean, how could you know how you're going to feel in 10 years? Or 20?"

Gram folded her apron in short, sharp movements, then slipped it into a drawer. Her face wore a look of exasperation. "Nikki, the only people in the world who could swallow that line are the ones who go around saying love is just some warm, fuzzy feeling. If that's the way you define love, then of course you feel free to walk out on a marriage when the feelings change—free to look for those feelings with someone else."

"So are you saying love *isn't* a feeling?"

"I'm saying, don't confuse the product of the thing with the thing itself! Love can give people wonderful feelings. But the feelings aren't all that love is."

Nikki thought about the feelings that almost overwhelmed her whenever she was with Jeff. *If that isn't love, then what is?*

Her puzzlement obviously showed on her face because Gram crossed the kitchen to stand in front of her, so close that Nikki could smell the fresh, sweet scent of roses she always associated with her grandmother, and launched into an explanation that was unusually long for her. "When you're done reading all those verses about divorce, Nikki, try reading 1 Corinthians 13." Gram smiled, but there was a sadness in her eyes. "You won't get a decent definition of love from all the movies and TV you see, or from most of the books you read. But you'll find it there, in just a few verses. And you'll find out that love is a decision—a decision to always do what's best for someone else. Does that make sense to you?"

"I'm not sure," Nikki began.

"Nikki, *think*. When two people say those marriage vows, they're making a covenant before God, promising to do some things for always. If love is just a feeling, then they're promising to have warm, fuzzy feelings about each other for as long as they live. But most of us can't promise how we'll feel 10 minutes from now, let alone 50 or 60 years down the road. No marriage can survive with that definition of love. Love has to be more than the feelings it gives."

Nikki sighed and slipped off the counter to her feet. "Maybe if I could have said that to Dad the way you just did, maybe he would have understood. Maybe he would have changed his mind."

The rose scent grew stronger as Gram put her arms around Nikki and held her close. "Honey, real love is a choice you make," she said, speaking softly against Nikki's hair. "Not something that just happens to you. But you have to understand that only your father can make that choice now. You can't make it for him, and you can't force him to make it by how you act or what you say.

"And you *especially* can't take responsibility for whatever choice he makes. Do you hear me?" Gram stepped back just enough so that Nikki could look into her eyes, which were filling with tears. "*You* are not responsible for getting your parents back together! Understand?"

∞

Back in her bedroom, Nikki curled up on the window seat, Bible open on her lap to 1 Corinthians 13. But instead of reading, she found herself watching as the sun sank with painstaking slowness into the gray-blue water of the lake.

If only Jeff were here now, she thought. *Jeff would listen. Jeff would talk through the whole thing with me—the conversation with Dad, all this stuff Gram's telling me—*

She sighed and pulled her thoughts up short. *Get real. Jeff would be telling me about Shannon, that's what he'd be doing!*

The sense of loss overwhelmed her. Jeff had been her truest friend, but now that was over. Just two nights ago she'd been so sure that praying would work out everything with Jeff, everything with her parents. Instead, things seemed much worse. So what was the use of praying, anyway?

Nikki snapped her Bible shut and grabbed her Spanish assignment as though there was nothing else she would rather do. Homework would take her mind off everything else. She could read 1 Corinthians later.

She was searching her English-Spanish dictionary for the word *oven* to complete the final sentence of her assignment—a one-page essay in Spanish on how to perform an everyday task, for which she'd chosen to write, "How to Bake Chocolate Chip Cookies"— when the phone rang. She went to the hall and picked it up.

"Nikki! All right!" Keesha's voice bubbled with excitement. "I just got Steve's e-mail! I *knew* you'd come around, I *knew* it! We are gonna have such a great time on Friday! The guys are planning to take us to Angelino's!"

"Keesha, what are you talking about?" Nikki took the phone back into her bedroom and shut the door.

There was a pause, then Keesha's voice went flat. "Oh, right. Play dumb, Nik. You're so funny."

Nikki dropped onto the bed, staring at the ceiling. "Keesha? I don't get what you mean. I wrote to Mitch on Sunday night, but it was just a kind of 'let's get to know each other' message. So what's all the excitement about?" She rested one ankle on top of the bent knee of her other leg, tracing O's in the air with pointed toes as she waited.

"I'm not playing your game, Nikki." Keesha sounded downright irritated now. "I got all excited about us going out together with the guys and now you're pretending you don't know anything. I *hate* it when you act this way! Call me when you're ready to talk."

Nikki swung her feet to the floor and sat up. There was a *click*, and the phone went dead.

She glared at the phone. *This is stupid.* She poked in Keesha's number and waited for her to pick up. When she did, Nikki tried to explain.

"Listen to me, Keesha Riley! I don't have a clue what you're talking about, okay?"

"Right. Like I believe that."

"Keesha!" Nikki was practically shouting with frustration now. "Would you please explain what's going on? I haven't even had a chance to see if Mitch wrote back yet. There's just been too much going on here."

"Listen, Nikki, all I know is that I got an e-mail from Steve saying—" She broke off. "Just go read your own e-mail, okay?" The phone went dead again.

Nikki sat on the edge of the bed for a minute, frowning, then made her way quietly downstairs to the study. The house was still and nearly dark, with only a faint glow from the street light casting window-shaped squares on the carpeted floor of the front hall. She scraped the study door over her bare big toe by accident as she swung it closed, and winced.

"Ow, ow, *ow!*" she hissed. She grabbed her toe, balancing herself on one foot like a flamingo until the pain subsided. When she could let go, she depressed the switch that turned on both the computer and the green-shaded desk lamp, then guided the cursor quickly through the steps to open her grandfather's e-mail account. She clicked the mouse quickly and brought up not one, but two messages addressed to her.

The first was the kind of reply she'd expected. Mitch answered all her questions, told her a lot about himself, and mentioned three times how much he was looking forward to meeting her. The letter ended with an invitation.

Steve and Keesha have another date for Friday night, and we all want to make it a foursome. We'll start at Angelino's for dinner, and then just let things happen from there. Just say yes, Nikki. Please.

That at least made sense, Nikki thought. *He answered my letter, then asked me out.* She clicked on the next message, which she hadn't expected. The words made no sense at first; she leaned forward, brows drawn together, scrutinizing the screen.

SUBJECT: Can't wait for Friday night!
Hey, Nikki,

> *Finally gonna give me a chance, huh? You won't be sorry, I promise you that. I couldn't believe it when I read your e-mail. Steve and I will get to Grand Rapids by six o'clock. We get out of school around three, so give us three hours to get there. We'll meet you and Keesha at Angelino's, which Steve said is a really cool place. We'll show you ladies a night you'll never forget. Count on that!*

> > *—Mitch*

Nikki stared at the words on the screen. *What gave Mitch the idea I said yes to Friday night?*

She wished she knew more about e-mail. Remembering the Internet lesson Keesha had given Grandpa, Nikki scanned the bar at the side of the screen. She clicked on SENT, then scrolled through the items listed. Several messages were Grandpa's, all before last Sunday. Then came her own letter to Mitch on Sunday night.

After that, dated September 6, at 9:17 P.M., there was another note to Mitch. Nikki frowned and clicked on the message.

Dear Mitch,

> *It was really sweet of you to ask me to come along on Friday night. I'd really like to go. I'll do my best to make it a night you'll never forget, too!*

> > *Love,*
> > *Nikki*

Nikki fell back in the chair and wondered, for a split second or so, if she could be losing her mind. There was the letter, right in front of her, signed with her name. She couldn't argue with the evidence. But she had no memory of ever writing it. Then she read it again, and winced at the last line. She would never have said that. *And I wouldn't have signed it 'Love, Nikki' either!*

She crossed her arms. *How did the message get there? Who wrote it, and why?* Whatever the answer, she had to get rid of these messages before Grandpa saw them. She didn't want to have to explain who Mitch was, and why she was writing him.

She clicked DELETE, then peered at the question that popped up: "Are you sure you want to delete this item permanently?" With a quick click on YES, she watched the message disappear.

She did the same with the other note, then tried to think back to Monday night at 9:17. Hadn't she been down at the dock, either still talking to Jeff in the boat, or standing around looking at Dr. Allen's monster bass? Jeff had been there too, of course, and Grandpa—not that either one of them could be a suspect.

Suddenly, Marlene Allen's worried face flashed through her mind. Nikki remembered how concerned Marlene had been because she couldn't find the twins.

So that's what they were doing. Nikki could just picture Abby, with her penchant for anything romantic, writing this letter and signing it "Love, Nikki." But that meant they'd been snooping around in Grandpa's e-mail and actually reading private letters. She'd have to deal with that later. It was too late now to call Allens.

Keesha was a different matter, though. Nikki picked up the phone on her grandfather's desk and punched in Keesha's number as fast as she could. The line was busy.

Over the next five minutes, she hit redial again and again, but the result was always the same.

Keesha must be online, probably talking to Steve. Meanwhile, I'd better write to Mitch and straighten this out.

The message to Mitch turned out to be harder than she expected. Trying to explain who the twins were and what they were doing in Nikki's grandfather's e-mail got awfully involved. Hardest of all was telling him that no, she did *not* plan to go out with him on Friday.

She wrote three versions, deleting each one as unsatisfactory. Finally, on the fourth try, Nikki knew she had to send it—whether or not it was exactly what she meant to say. She ended the message by turning down the date in the most unoffensive way she could think of.

> *I really don't have any plans for Friday night at this point. Hope you'll understand.*
>
> *Nikki*

Once the screen reported her mail had been sent, she shut down the computer and went upstairs, too agitated to read 1 Corinthians 13, or Psalms, or even the English-Spanish dictionary to find the word *oven*.

❧ *Thirteen* ❧

THE NEXT MORNING, NIKKI pulled on her clothes in a rush and skipped breakfast in order to get to school in time to talk to Keesha before homeroom.

She wheeled the Mazda into the student parking lot, then hurried through the double glass doors and up the stairs to the second floor. Keesha was already at her locker, dressed in a tie-dyed, orange T-shirt and jean shorts, squatting before the open door, searching the navy blue backpack that sat open on the locker floor.

"Keesha! Wait'll I tell you what happened. You're never going to believe this." Nikki launched into her description of what had to be Abby's e-mail to Mitch.

To her surprise, however, Keesha stood up and whirled around, her expression angry.

Nikki stopped in mid-sentence. "*What* is your *problem*, Keesha Riley?"

"Sounds like a pretty easy out for you, that's all I can say." Keesha's hands rested squarely on her hips as she glared at Nikki.

"What are you talking about?"

"You go sending all these e-mails to Mitch, leading him on, making Steve think we're all going out together. Then you just change your tune. And blame it on a little kid, yet!" Keesha stooped to get her backpack.

"You're saying I'm *lying* here?" Nikki demanded.

Keesha gave a derisive *hmmph*.

Nikki turned toward her own locker, trying not to let her anger go out of control. "What possible, logical reason would I have to lie about this? Would you just tell me that?" Spinning the combination, she noted with relief that the locker door now opened.

"How should I know?" Keesha said. "I just don't see any point in being friends with someone who does."

Nikki shoved her Spanish book and notebook onto the shelf and faced her friend. "Keesha, please! I'm trying to explain what happened. How am I supposed to do that if you won't listen and you won't talk sense?"

But Keesha was in no mood to talk. She found whatever it was she'd been searching for, then zipped the backpack and flung it over her shoulder. "Figure it out yourself, Einstein," she said, slamming the locker door and taking off down the hall toward homeroom.

"Keesha!" Nikki called after her. "Keesha, wait a minute! I need to discuss this with you!"

"Forget it, Nik!"

Nikki watched helplessly as the back of Keesha's tie-dyed, orange shirt disappeared around the corner. Feeling totally childish, she nevertheless gave into her frustration and yelled down the now-empty hall, "Fine, then! Be that way! See if I care!" Then she slammed her own locker door as hard as she could.

As the echo of the locker door died away, the stillness of the hall seemed to ring in her ears. Then, from behind her, came the click of a door latch. A classroom door opened just far enough to reveal Hollis McCaffrey's pained-looking face, with Noel Jacobs peering over her shoulder. They both stared at Nikki, then up and down the empty hall, then back at her.

"Look. Excuse me," Hollis said in her carefully modulated voice. "But would you mind keeping your voice down, Nikki? We're having a yearbook meeting in here and we're right in the middle of an important discussion. That is, we *were* in the middle of it." Hollis's brown eyebrows disappeared upward into the brown, spiky bangs that covered her forehead.

All Nikki could do was nod wordlessly, hoping her cheeks weren't as red as they felt.

Nikki could hardly hear what was going on in her classes through the thoughts of her parents, and Jeff and Shannon, and now, Keesha. Over and over through the day, she tried to force the confusion away and pay attention in class. Last year this time, she'd been totally distracted with thoughts of the baby she was carrying, with the weight of all the decisions she was being forced to make. But this year was supposed to be her time to catch up, academically, so she'd be ready to start college next year. And socially, so she could have a life again. But it wasn't working. And on top of everything else, there was the matter of this speech for Arleta's tea . . . She swallowed hard, remembering that it was only four days away now and she had absolutely nothing prepared.

Nikki had two immediate goals when she got home that afternoon.

Number one: Get to the study and check Grandpa's e-mail. After all the talk about the possible dangers of the Web, she'd feel like a fool if he saw an e-mail from Mitch that made it look as though she was picking up some guy she'd met online.

Number two: Get some time alone on the beach and figure out what to say in the speech.

She cut the engine of the Mazda, grabbed her backpack, and hurried up the back steps. As soon as she stepped inside the kitchen, however, she knew it would be at least a while before she got to either of those goals.

Rachel was sitting at the kitchen table. When Nikki entered the room, Rachel gestured toward one of the chairs and reached for a pitcher of iced tea. "Would you like some tea, Nicole?"

Nikki shot a last glance at the doorway that led to the hall. "Um, I don't think so, Mother. I have some things I really need to get to—"

Rachel's fingers closed on the handle of the glass pitcher. "Please.

I'd just like to hear how school is going for you, if you can spare a few minutes."

Nikki felt caught. That vulnerability was there again in Rachel's face, that tinge of some new openness that had been there on Sunday night when they looked at Evan's pictures together.

She settled into the chair her mother had offered. "Maybe I would like some tea, after all."

Rachel questioned her about classes as Nikki drank; Nikki gave all the answers she felt safe telling. Long years of disagreements and misunderstandings between them left her cautious enough to keep back details such as the hall confrontation with Hollis and Noel, and especially Chad's comments.

And there's no way I'm bringing up this whole Mitch situation with her, Nikki said silently, trying not to think about what Grandpa might be reading in the study at that very moment.

After 15 minutes the conversation seemed to be winding down. Nikki gathered her books together and drained the last of her tea. Rachel, however, clearly had something else on her mind. She stretched out a hand to touch Nikki's arm.

"Nikki, there is something else I'd like to say to you."

Nikki set her glass on the table top and waited.

"Yesterday, when your father was here, I . . . said some things. Some of them were very . . . impolite. I thought a lot last night about what your grandmother said, that no good would come from putting you in the middle. And—well, I think she's right."

You *think someone* else *is right?* Nikki stared at her, waiting.

Rachel acknowledged Nikki's surprise with a slight lift of her eyebrows, and the perfect shell-pink ovals of her fingernails clicked against the sides of her tea glass. "To be honest, I'm not sure exactly how to behave toward your father, given the circumstances. But what I did yesterday—that wasn't it. I . . . wanted to say I'm . . . sorry. For calling him an idiot."

Shame washed over Nikki as she sat listening. *I'm supposed to be the Christian here,* she thought. *But here I was thinking things so much worse than what you said!*

Sudden feeling for her mother welled up inside her. It was an emotion so strong Nikki had to look away, clearing her throat to divert attention from what was going on inside.

It had been so long since she'd felt this way about her mother that it took a few seconds before she could even identify the feeling—as love.

When she finished talking with her mother, Nikki was relieved to find her grandfather's study vacant, though the computer was on. A school of fantastically-colored tropical fish now swam back and forth across the monitor, replacing the pipe screen saver Grandpa usually had on.

Sliding into his desk chair, she sent the fish into oblivion with a click of the mouse. Quickly she called up the e-mail screen. There was a message, but it was addressed to OLDBIO. The subject line read, "More Info. from Monterey Bay Aquarium."

She gave a sigh of relief and slipped out of the office to the beach. At least there she would have the chance to work on this speech, where no phones would ring—and she wouldn't have to worry about e-mail.

"I just want to take this opportunity to say that I'm really honored to be here today—"

Nikki broke off, kicking her bare toe at the pebbly sand. *That won't work. Sounds like I'm accepting Player of the Year Award at some sports banquet.*

"I'd just like to say thank you—" She broke off again and started to giggle. When speakers in church or school assemblies used that phrase, something in her always wanted to yell, "So say it, already! Just say it!" because she had noticed that they rarely did. The idea of saying that in front of a group of women was just too funny.

Nikki climbed up the boulders onto the pier and stared out toward the end. As far as she could see, she had the pier totally to herself. Sunshine warmed her bare arms and feet, and she stretched her hands high above her head for a minute, luxuriating in the feel of it.

The sun was gentler these days, less intense. Autumn was definitely on the way. She walked the length of the pier and sat at the very end, dangling her feet over the crumbling concrete edge.

Okay, think, she told herself, a feeling of desperation starting to grow. *I can leave the opening sentence till later. For right now, I just have to figure out the rest of what I want to say.* She knew she could do it, given time and quiet. So why wouldn't any ideas come?

Arleta expects me to talk about getting pregnant with Evan, but what am I supposed to tell these people, anyway? About what it feels like when a guy gets what he wants from you, then never even speaks to you again?

Or when you know—deep down in the pit of your stomach—that you missed your last period because something different is going on inside you, something you never expected to experience for a long, long time?

Nikki pried loose some of the pebbles in the concrete and aimed them, one by one, at a piece of slimy, green algae floating near the base of the pier. *How about what it's like the first day you go to school and it's obvious you've got a gut you never had before? And people kind of look at you sideways, then their eyes slide away real quick?*

She remembered Hollis doing exactly that in Spanish last fall— so many times, in fact, that Nikki felt an almost overwhelming urge to get right in her face and say, "So *ask* me already, would you? Just quit beating around the bush and ask me!"

Pressure built up inside her chest at the memories of last year. There was no way she could talk about this stuff in front of people. Unless—

A kind of craziness took hold of her. Giggling at the thought of Arleta's reaction, she started listing all the things she *could* talk about, if she had the nerve. *Heartburn. Stretch marks. Prenatal vitamins, constipation, watching the needle on the scale creep upward to numbers I never thought I'd see. Lamaze classes and breathing exercises, labor, adoption papers—*

Nikki pried off a jagged chunk of concrete and let it fall straight down with a *plunk* into the dark water beneath her feet. Suddenly she didn't feel like laughing anymore. In all the confusion of the last few days, she'd hardly prayed for Evan, something she'd vowed to do every day of her life. Pregnancy and other people's reactions to it might have a funny side, but there was nothing funny about being responsible for starting a whole new life. Especially one she couldn't even take care of.

She remembered the way tiny Evan had nestled in her arms at the adoption ceremony. She recalled how it felt to hand him to the Shiveleys, his adoptive parents, knowing he would never truly be hers again.

She'd gone just a few weeks ago for her six-month visit with him. Evan had been sitting in his high chair in the Shiveleys' kitchen, drooling happily all over the Zwieback® cookie he was gumming.

"Oh, Nikki, I'm sorry," Marilyn Shiveley apologized, embarrassed. "I had him all clean for you, honestly. It's just that he's cutting a tooth on top there and all he wants to do is bite on things. He's been drooling this way for a week now."

But Nikki hardly noticed the drooling or the cookie paste smeared all over Evan's chin and bib. What she noticed was the impassive way he glanced at her, curious only because hers was an unfamiliar face. Then he fixed his eyes on Marilyn once again, following her every move. When Marilyn left the room to get him more juice, he pulled the cookie from his mouth and made loud noises, almost a series of yells. It was obvious he was trying to call her back.

Nikki was happy to see him thriving and well cared for. But she hadn't quite been prepared to see with her own eyes that Marilyn was now his mother. And Nikki—Nikki was a stranger.

That part wasn't funny at all.

Nikki pulled her knees against her chest, wrapping her arms around them. Then she bowed her head and began to pray for Evan.

It was Gallie who found her there, poking his soft, golden snout underneath her arm again and again, nudging at her until she lifted her head and he could see her face. He licked her cheek, a great, wet, sloppy kiss that made her laugh and push him away at the same time. "Go on, you crazy mutt!" She rubbed his ears and patted his forehead, all the while keeping her face out of reach.

"Quite the tracking dog, isn't he?" Rachel asked as she stopped at the end of the pier beside Nikki. "He brought me right to you."

Nikki gave a short laugh and shielded her eyes from the sun with her hand so she could look up. "Oh, yeah! He tracked me down, all right, hidden out here in full view of the whole world. What are you—I mean, why are you down here?" Her words were awkward with surprise.

Nikki could count on one hand the times she'd seen her mother on the pier. She tried to sound more welcoming. "You want to sit down?" She gestured at the pier beside her.

Rachel shrugged slightly, then lowered herself gracefully to the cement beside Nikki. "I've been holed up in the house forever, so I decided to get some fresh air. And I noticed you—or rather, Gallie brought you to my attention. You've been out here quite a while, Nikki. Is everything okay?"

Nikki nodded. "I guess so. I'm just trying to figure out what on earth to say at the tea on Sunday. I don't really think I'm cut out to be a public speaker, you know?"

Rachel drew her knees up to her chest and leaned her chin on them, staring down into the water. "I heard someone say once that public speaking is the number one fear of American adults. It even beats out cancer and dying, if I remember correctly."

"Oh, yeah? Well, I understand, believe me." Gallie trotted up to sit between them, a stick in his mouth, looking back and forth from one to the other.

Nikki rubbed the dog's floppy ears. "Ready for another swim, huh? I don't think so, boy, not way out here. One dive in this 30-foot water and we'd have to call the Coast Guard to haul you out." Gallie flopped down between them with a dog sigh, his disappointment obvious.

The silence stretched long between them before Nikki finally spoke again. "I guess the real reason I've been out here so long is that I was thinking about Evan. Thinking and praying."

Nikki almost looked around to see whether someone else had said the words. Suddenly she found herself wanting to share things with Rachel that she had never dreamed she'd be able to say.

Rachel glanced sideways at her, then back to the water. "I can't imagine what it must be like for you, giving him up. I could never—" She broke off and swallowed, then picked up in a more everyday tone. "You said you were praying for Evan?"

Nikki nodded.

"Is that something you do often?"

"I try to do it every day. I don't always make it, but I'm trying."

Rachel stretched her legs down the side of the cement pier and leaned back on her hands, staring at the clouds. "But how would you know, Nikki?"

Nikki looked at her. "Know what?"

"If you got what you thought was an answer to your prayers, how would you know it wasn't just a coincidence?"

Her first response was to panic. How was she—still a new Christian—supposed to answer a question like that?

Then she laughed at a memory that popped into her head. "I don't know how to answer that," Nikki began, "because I don't think I've been a Christian long enough. But I remember something Aunt Marta said to me once. She'd heard somebody tell about an old man who said, 'All I know is, when I pray, coincidences happen a lot more often.' "

Rachel smiled shortly, then looked sober again. "Well, even if I did believe in a God like the one in the Bible, I don't think He's getting terribly involved with people these days. People like me, I mean. I know the old stories, about Moses and Joshua and all of them, but that was a long, long time ago."

She glanced at Nikki again, then laughed. "I know, I know! I grew up here, too, remember? And, contrary to what your grandparents think, I still remember a lot of the verses. 'Jesus Christ, the same yesterday, today, and forever,' right?"

Nikki nodded, thinking this was probably the first time in her life she'd ever heard Rachel talk about God with anything other than a sneer. "Well, we'll see what happens, Nikki. We'll see. The way things are right now, I'm certainly not above asking for a little divine intervention myself." She swung her legs back onto the pier to stand up.

"Mother? Before you go, there's something I need to say, if you have a minute." Nikki hesitated, almost hoping her mother would decline, but she only waited, watching her daughter expectantly.

"I don't know if it's the right time to talk to you about this, but I need to tell you I'm really sorry."

"Sorry for what, Nicole?"

"You said that Dad met this . . . this other woman . . . after I . . . after I got pregnant and all."

Rachel tipped her head a little in Nikki's direction. "Yes. He did, as far as I know."

"Well, I think that maybe that's why he did this. I disappointed him, you know? I wasn't what he hoped and—"

At first Rachel seemed to listen only casually. But then her eyes opened wide, and for the first time that week she seemed able to see beyond her own feelings. "Wait a minute!" she broke in. "Are you telling me you think that *you* are the cause of all this?"

Nikki nodded. "Yeah, kind of."

Rachel's gaze fixed on her. "Then you listen to me, Nicole Sheridan. *We* did this, your father and I. Not you, do you hear? Yes, your getting pregnant was hard for us, I won't deny that. But we made it harder by being concerned only for ourselves, how we would look to others, our reputation—that kind of thing. *We* were the ones who acted like children, putting ourselves at the center of everything and not even worrying about you."

She looked away and her voice dropped to a near whisper. "Or Evan." She looked back then and laid her hand on Nikki's knee. "I'm so sorry, Nikki."

Rachel stood up then and gave a shaky laugh. "This seems to be my day for apologizing, doesn't it?"

Nikki got to her feet, also, and looked into her mother's eyes. "Thank you for apologizing. And I want you to know, it's okay . . . Mom."

Though they could hear nothing different, Gallie sat bolt upright, cocking an ear toward shore. Then he was on his feet in a flash, loping the length of the pier. Rachel glanced back up the beach to where the blue clapboard house and the Allens' stained wood home sat on the cliff. She pointed at a lone figure standing at the head of the long ladder of beach stairs, waving a large square of yellow cloth.

"That'll be your grandmother, telling us to come home for dinner, Nikki."

They walked back to the house, this time side by side.

Fourteen

TRYING TO REMEMBER WHY she'd looked forward so much to being a senior, Nikki worked at her homework for several hours that night. The faint sound of voices drifted up from the screened porch below, where her grandparents and Rachel sat until about 10 o'clock.

When she heard them come upstairs and the house was quiet, Nikki made her way downstairs to the study to check the e-mail. She noted with relief that there was no communication from Mitch.

Instead, she toyed with the idea of writing to Keesha to see if they could work this thing out.

But she got only as far as *Dear Keesha* when the Instant Message box appeared. In it was a message from Mitch.

Hey, Nikki! Can't believe I actually caught you online!

Nikki typed back, feeling caught. *Yeah, isn't this something?* She waited for Mitch to respond.

I was just going to leave you a message to let you know how much I've been thinking about you, lady. But now we can talk for a minute, huh? Listen, I don't know what kind of weird stuff's going on over there. All I know is, I got a great message from you saying you'd come on Friday, and Steve and I made reservations at Angelino's and everything. You wouldn't want to let two great guys down, now would you?

Mitch, she wrote, *I don't think you understand, exactly. See, Keesha and I were just kind of goofing off last Saturday when I met you. I didn't mean to start anything here.*

Say no more! Mitch replied. *Keesha and I were talking online earlier this evening, and she explained it all to me how you're so shy and everything, and I understand. Believe it or not, I'm pretty shy myself. I mean, online I do okay, but you'll see when you meet me. I'm not so comfortable talking in person, either. So don't worry about Friday night, babe. We'll—*

Everything stopped dead at that point. Nikki rolled the mouse around and hit ESCAPE, but nothing happened and she realized the computer had frozen up. She switched everything off and got to her feet, fuming. Keesha's phone line was busy. *Of course*, she thought. *Probably, she's creating even wilder stories to tell Steve.*

"Wait till I see you tomorrow, Keesha Riley," she muttered.

Keesha was at her locker again when Nikki arrived at school the next morning. Nikki put her hands on her hips and looked at her through narrowed eyes, and Keesha shook her head.

"Uh-oh! Looks like you've been talking to Mitch, right? Now don't go getting all riled up at me again before you find out what's really going on, girl."

Nikki set the books for her afternoon classes on the shelf in her locker. "I'll think about that. And how about, in the meantime, you tell me what kind of story you actually told Mitch about me. *Shy* me, that is."

"Oh, come on, Nik," Keesha said, leaning forward toward her locker mirror, outlining her lips with a copper-colored lipstick pencil. "So I bent the truth a little. The point is, it saved my neck with Steve. He was getting really put out with me, you have to understand!"

"Put out about what?" Nikki crossed her arms over her chest and waited.

"Nikki, have a heart! You know how I feel about Steve. I can't lose him right now. He's the best thing in my life!" There was a pleading tone in Keesha's voice. *She'd do anything to keep Steve*, Nikki thought.

"I heard you the first time, Keesha. But you still haven't answered my question. What was Steve so 'put out' about that you had to lie?"

Obviously avoiding Nikki's gaze, Keesha squatted in front of her locker and started putting her books for the first half of the day inside her bag. "Look, Nikki. Steve really cares about me, you know? But Mitch is like his best friend in the world, and they've always done everything together. So the deal was, I was supposed to get Mitch a date, too, so they could come over together, okay? And when they thought you were backing out, Steve said maybe things weren't working out as well as he thought between him and me."

"Keesha, how could you? This is why you got me online with Mitch on Saturday? What about all that stuff about it being good for me to meet someone else because I was upset with Jeff? That was all lies?"

"Yes. I mean *no!* I meant that, Nikki. You do need to meet someone else and get your mind off Jeff. And now, you listen to me." She turned to face Nikki, pointing at her face. "The guy's crazy for you. Wait till you hear what he and Steve have planned for tomorrow night."

"It won't make a bit of difference, Keesha. Mitch may be the greatest guy in the world, but I'm still not going out with the three of you. Get it into your head already! And stop bothering me about it."

Keesha's black eyes flashed. "Nikki, would you use your brain? Jeff Allen drops you for some gorgeous blonde. You have absolutely nobody else in your life. But you won't even consider a guy like Mitch, just because you met him over a computer wire instead of a phone wire! I think you need to find out where you stand with Jeff, so you can make up your mind—"

Nikki never heard the rest, because Hollis and Noel turned the hall corner toward them at just that moment. "Nikki," Hollis called, "we've decided to come and hear you on Sunday."

Nikki nodded and tried to make her smile look gracious. "Good. I'm glad."

But her heart sank at the words, then fell even lower as Hollis continued. "We got some of our friends to come, too."

Nikki ran a nervous hand though her long, curly hair, lifted it from underneath, then let it fall back into place. "Oh. Great. I hope— you enjoy it."

"Well, enjoy isn't really the word, you know?" Hollis gave a short, humorless laugh and blinked at Nikki over the tops of her glasses. "A couple of us were discussing the whole abortion thing this summer. We're pretty hopelessly divided, so we think the best thing we can do is listen to someone who's gone the other way— having the baby, I mean."

She said "having the baby" as though she couldn't quite imagine why *anyone, anywhere* would actually do such a thing. As Hollis and Noel walked on, Nikki wished she could crawl inside her locker and pull the brown metal door shut behind her—at least until Arleta's tea was over.

That evening, as Grandpa lifted his head from saying grace over dinner, Rachel announced her plans to return to Ohio on Saturday morning.

Gram and Grandpa expressed concern about her leaving so soon to go back to the empty house in Millbrook. For a second Nikki could see a look of bleakness in her mother's eyes, before the old in-control expression fell back into place. "I may as well go Satur- day," Rachel said. "I have to be there to start teaching next Monday. Millions of women have gotten through this. I'm sure I will, too."

Maybe I should go back with her, Nikki thought. *I could move into the house there in Millbrook.*

But she knew that wouldn't work. Life had changed too dras- tically in the past year; Michigan was home now. Gram and Grandpa were more family than her parents had been for years. Still, she caught herself feeling reluctant to let go of the new Rachel she felt she was just getting to know.

"I thought maybe you'd stay for the tea on Sunday," Nikki said tentatively. "To hear me speak, you know?"

Rachel shook her head. "I thought about it. And I really would have liked to. But I've got too much preparation to leave it all till the day before classes start." She looked into Nikki's eyes. "I am sorry to miss hearing you, really."

While it wasn't all she'd hoped, Nikki thought, it was something, to have Rachel apologize as though her heart was in it. "You'll miss the Allens, too," she added. "They're coming back for the weekend, remember?"

"I know. But I really should get back." Rachel's words were dogged, but lacked any sense of conviction.

Nikki poked her thick slice of London broil with her fork, then spoke quietly. "I wish you would stay. But if you can't, I'll help you pack tomorrow night. If you'd like, I mean."

Rachel nodded, and the corners of her mouth turned up slightly. "I would, Nikki. Thank you."

Nikki spent the rest of the evening in her room, rushing through all her homework at breakneck speed so she could work on the speech. Over and over, she saw Hollis's face and heard her words, and felt the pressure of saying something convincing about abortion, something that would have impact. She remembered the feel of Evan kicking inside her, the sound of his heart beating strongly on the monitor. How could she ever come up with words to explain *that?*

At the sight of Jeff standing at the sceen door at dinnertime on Friday, Nikki's feelings almost overwhelmed her. *Finally!* she thought. She'd been edgy with worry ever since he'd called at three that afternoon to say he was stuck in a massive traffic jam on I–96.

"There's a tractor-trailer full of pigs overturned just west of Lansing," he'd explained, his voice crackling with static, "and it's blocking both lanes. What? No, I'm not kidding! We're all out of our cars, just standing around, and the guy who's parked ahead of me is letting me use his car phone to call you. You'll tell my parents where I am when they get there?"

"Here, you can tell them yourself. Your mother's standing right here in the kitchen. I understand they got here about noon, but I haven't seen your dad or the twins yet because a certain doctor wanted to do more fishing, you know?" Nikki had been laughing a little as she started to hand the phone to Marlene Allen, but she didn't like to think of Jeff and accidents at the same time. She put the phone back against her ear and added, "You be careful, you hear?"

Now Jeff stood in front of her, safe and sound, and for just a second, all her concerns about Shannon were swept away. For the moment, there was only Jeff as she'd always known him. Jeff with the deep blue, thickly-lashed eyes that sparkled when he saw her, Jeff with the legs so long he had to look down at even his father and Grandpa these days. And most of all, Jeff, her best friend, and the one person she knew she was growing to care about more deeply each day.

She tucked the back tail of her plaid, sleeveless shirt into her white shorts and motioned with her head for him to come in. "Since when do you knock? Come on, get in here," she told him, laughing to cover her emotion.

He pushed the door open, looking at her as he did. "Hey, I like that shirt on you. Looks good." He stopped and frowned. "Come here for a minute though." She took a step toward him and he stretched one arm around the back of her neck. She felt the warmth of his fingers at her collar and smelled the sweet scent of his cologne. "You might want to learn to wear your tags inside, okay?"

Nikki waved him away, trying to ignore the sudden storm of feelings she had at his unexpected nearness. "Ready to go?" she asked.

"You bet I am. All I could think about the whole time I was stuck in that crazy traffic jam was eating Rosie's burritos."

They sat on the patio behind Rosie's, watching gulls swoop low over Lake Michigan as they ate, and Jeff once again got her laughing with stories about life at U of M. Frequently, however, Nikki caught herself losing focus on what he was saying. No matter how much she wanted to just enjoy being with Jeff, two things kept interfering. Shannon was definitely her biggest concern. All week long she'd worried and wondered, and now she kept hearing Keesha's words echo in her mind. *You better find out where you stand with Jeff,* she had said, and Nikki knew she was right. She couldn't imagine living through another week like this one, never knowing how Jeff really felt.

Beyond Shannon, though, her thoughts kept wandering off, irritatingly, to Keesha, who had tried right up till the end of the day at school to persuade her to change her mind about going with Steve and Mitch. "Mitch is coming, no matter what you say. Steve says it's my job to get you there, so come on, Nik. We'll have a great time." Nikki had had no problem refusing, in light of the fact that she knew she'd be meeting Jeff, and she even threw in a few pointed comments to needle Keesha about picking up guys off the Internet.

They had resolved their differences about Steve and Mitch to the point where they could disagree and still laugh about it. Even so, a faint uneasiness kept drifting across her thoughts, like the wispy cirrus clouds that dimmed the sun almost imperceptibly on a summer day.

Jeff finally leaned forward and waved a hand in front of her. "Am I boring you?"

Nikki laughed and apologized.

"I'm losing you every couple of minutes here, Nikki." His eyes were warm with sympathy. "I guess I'd be far away too, if my mind was on my parents the way yours must be."

She didn't correct him. It would take too much effort to explain about Keesha. And if she did, Nikki would then be forced to explain how she had gotten involved in the whole situation. In one way, she couldn't help wanting to meet Mitch, true. He'd been very attentive and romantic online. But in another way, she wished now that she'd never talked with Mitch online, and she certainly didn't want to explain that part to Jeff. And there was no use trying to explain how Mitch had gotten an e-mail supposedly from her, agreeing to go out with him, because Jeff would be furious with the twins for what they'd done. Nikki preferred to deal with Abby and Adam herself, privately, as long as they gave her their word they would never get involved in this kind of situation again.

Nikki finished off the last bits of her burrito and wiped the corners of her mouth. What she needed to do was go somewhere where she could get her mind off Keesha and finally talk the whole issue of Shannon out with Jeff. "Jeff, you may not get back to Rosendale for quite a while after this weekend. Let's go take one last walk on the beach. Want to?"

On their short drive back to the house, Nikki thought frantically how she could bring up the issue of Shannon. *I thought if I waited long enough, Jeff would do it himself, but I was wrong.* She winced at the thought of doing this, even though she knew she had to. *I'm going to make a total idiot of myself, I know it. He's never liked jealous girls, either.*

Jeff parked the Bronco in the Allens' driveway and called through the open screen door to his mother, who was standing in front of the open refrigerator, a rag in hand. "Nik and I'll be down on the beach. See you in a bit!"

They walked toward the beach steps together, and Nikki took a deep breath and began. "Jeff, there's something I've been wanting to talk to you about all week, but I just didn't feel comfortable bringing it up."

Jeff looked at her in surprise, then motioned for her to go ahead of him down the stairs. "Nik, there's nothing we can't talk about. You know that. So what's on your mind?"

"I think we need to talk about—well, about—"

"*Jeff! Jeff, hold on!*" Marlene Allen's voice called from the kitchen doorway. "You have a phone call!"

Jeff sighed. "Walk back with me, would you, Nik? This may be something important."

I'm important! Nikki wanted to scream, but Jeff was already loping back across the yard toward his mother. He took the cordless phone from her hand and spoke for a moment, then looked up apologetically, just as Nikki arrived at his side. He pushed the HOLD button.

"It's *Shannon*, Nikki. I have to talk to her. This can't wait. You don't mind, do you?"

At that point, something seemed to explode inside Nikki. "No. Of *course* I don't mind. Why would I mind, Jeffrey Allen? I've only been trying to talk to you all week long about this, but no. That doesn't matter, does it? I think you *should* talk to Shannon, by all means. Just don't talk to me ever again, you got that?"

Jeff's dark blue eyes opened wide and he shook his head back and forth. "Wait a minute, Nikki, you don't understand what's—"

"*I* don't understand? What do you think I am, some kind of *imbecile?* I understand *perfectly!*" Nikki's voice was loud enough that Marlene Allen had come back to the kitchen door and stood watching her, but Nikki's outrage edged out any feelings of embarrassment she would normally have had. It felt as though everything that had gone wrong this entire week had just come to a head, and there was no way of keeping it inside. She turned and stormed toward her grandparents' house. Inside, she could hear her grandparents and Arleta—who must have come by while she was out with Jeff, she thought, talking on the back porch. She stayed just long enough to grab her car keys, then saw a message on the counter, addressed to her. She picked up the yellow sticky and squinted at Grandpa's scrawl.

Keesha called. Says please change your mind. Also says Mitch is gorgeous.

Beneath the lines, two question marks stood side by side in parentheses, Grandpa's way of teasing her, she knew. *Some questions you're better off not having answered, Grandpa,* she thought, relieved that he wasn't around to ask in person. He would never understand.

She left through the front door, hoping to avoid the sight of Jeff on the phone with Shannon. Jeff saw her head toward her car though, and hollered in her direction. "Nikki, wait a minute! Where are you going?"

"Out with somebody who *wants* to be with me, okay?"

She started the Mazda and backed out of the driveway as fast as she dared, then headed the car toward Angelino's. It was almost as if the decision had been made for her, a decision she should have made days ago. With Mitch, she wouldn't have to wonder if his mind was on her or some other girl. Mitch *wanted* to take her out.

It wasn't until she was several minutes down the road that the first misgivings hit.

What about telling Keesha that this could be dangerous, meeting strangers on the Internet? She brushed the thought aside. She'd always been too cautious about everything. Other people—like Keesha, for instance—didn't worry about every bad possibility. Not only had nothing bad happened to Keesha, she'd finally found the relationship she'd been looking for.

Weren't you all excited about praying for Jeff and seeing what happened?

That one was harder to handle. She didn't want to say it out loud; in fact, it was hard to even think it. But inside, Nikki knew she had changed her mind and decided to handle this one on her own.

✦ Fifteen ✦

ANGELINO'S IS A PUBLIC PLACE, Nikki told herself as she drove. *What could happen in a restaurant, after all?*

She gripped the steering wheel a little harder, trying to ignore the apprehension that tingled through her.

The parking lot was nearly empty when she reached it, but she was expecting that. Angelino's was always packed during the tourist season, but once school started it was nearly deserted. In November the owners would hang a CLOSED sign on the door and take off for Tampa until May.

Shutting off the engine, Nikki looked around uneasily. The lot was almost totally shielded from view of the road by a thick stand of trees. *I never noticed that before,* she thought. When she'd been here before, her attention had been on the panoramic view of Lake Michigan and the Italian specialties for which Angelino's was famous.

She hesitated in the doorway of the restaurant, letting her eyes adjust to the soft semi-darkness. On the tables candles flickered in red glass globes, and only their faint light augmented the last of the sunshine from the tinted windows that lined the lake side of the restaurant.

A tiny, small-boned woman with blond hair piled elegantly on top of her head—and the highest heels Nikki thought she had ever seen—emerged from the kitchen. "My apologies," she murmured, in an accent so slight it barely colored her words. "I did not see you come in. How many?"

Nikki laughed nervously. "I'm alone. I mean, I'm here to meet some friends. I mean, they're not really friends, two of them, but—"

At the sight of the hostess's overly polite smile and raised eyebrow, Nikki broke off, aware of how foolish she sounded. "Never mind. Could you just help me find the people I'm supposed to meet?" She described Keesha, and gave the few details she knew about Steve and Mitch.

The waitress nodded as Nikki finished. "Yes, I think I know which ones you mean," she said. "They are around the corner, by the windows." She led the way to a secluded area with an unobstructed view of Lake Michigan.

Nikki walked across the dark carpet to the booth where Keesha sat with two guys. "So, am I late?" she asked brightly.

Keesha looked up, startled. Then she squealed. "Guys! This is her—Nikki Sheridan!"

For a moment Keesha frowned and lowered her voice. "What are you doing here, Nik? You said you weren't going to come. Anyway, that doesn't matter now—you can tell me later." She smiled again, and resumed normal volume. "Here, meet Steve."

The African-American guy who had been squeezed tightly against Keesha's side stood up. He seemed to tower over the booth, and Nikki put him at well over six feet.

"Hey, Nikki," Steve said offhandedly.

She remembered Keesha's delighted description of his wide shoulders, his huge biceps, his height. *At least she got the last part right,* Nikki thought. Apart from his height, the romantic Steve looked unremarkable to her.

The guy on the other side of the booth got to his feet as well. "And this is Mitch," announced Keesha.

"Hi," Mitch said softly, and slid over to make room for her. He was slighter than Steve, and stood maybe 5' 9" or 10", she estimated. Her glance took in his dark brown hair, pulled back into a ponytail. His chin was a little too long, the cleft a bit too pronounced.

Nowhere near as good-looking as Jeff, was her first reaction, but she pushed it away angrily.

"We already ate, Nik," Keesha said. "Dessert'll be here any minute. But you can still order dinner."

"Oh, no, that's okay," Nikki said. She could still feel the burrito from Rosie's sitting in her stomach like a rock.

"Come on," Steve urged. "You've gotta have something. The food is awesome here."

She decided to compromise. "I'll have a salad."

As they began to eat, Nikki wondered why Keesha had been so impressed with Mitch. But as he began to talk, she had to admit there was a certain shy charm about him.

He seemed to have a way, Nikki soon discovered, of drawing her out by asking questions. He asked if she'd grown up in West Michigan, and listened as she explained that she was actually from Ohio. He followed up some of the questions he'd asked via e-mail about her interests, and he asked about the car she drove and the subjects she liked in school.

It all seemed pleasant enough, Nikki thought after the first half hour or so, except . . . She couldn't quite put her finger on it, but somehow Mitch's interest in her didn't seem quite real.

Don't get paranoid, Nikki, she told herself. *You just met the guy, and he's probably nervous, too.* But it was more than that, and she knew it.

Steve excused himself to go to the men's room and was gone for several minutes. After he came back, Nikki began to realize that she didn't know any more about Steve and Mitch than she had when she'd sat down. The entire time she had been there, the guys had only asked questions about Keesha and herself, never volunteering anything about themselves.

She tried to turn the tables.

"Mitch, you said on e-mail that you were really into computers. What exactly did you mean?"

Mitch suddenly sounded defensive. "I meant what anybody would mean when they say that. Why are you asking?"

Nikki swirled a leaf of romaine lettuce through the last of the dressing on her plate. "I guess I just wanted to get to know you better, that's all."

"Oh, I wouldn't worry about that," Mitch answered.

Nikki frowned. "*What?*"

Steve shot an irritated glance at Mitch, then looked across the table at Nikki. "He just means there'll be plenty of time to get to know him better."

Nikki felt a twinge of uneasiness. "So, what *do* you do with computers?"

"We write programs," Mitch answered. "For games."

"Go on! You *write* them? What kind of games?" Keesha asked, obviously impressed.

Steve shrugged modestly and leaned back in his seat. "All kinds. We did one once that was kind of a takeoff on Dungeons and Dragons™—you have heard of Dungeons and Dragons™, right?"

"Well, of course!" Keesha said. "This is really exciting! I never met anybody who actually wrote computer games all by themselves."

Steve picked up his soda glass. "We don't actually write them alone, Keesha. We have kind of a group of guys back in Detroit that we work with."

"Like a computer club?" Keesha asked. "In your school or something?"

Steve laughed suddenly, almost choking on his soda. "No, Keesha," he said finally, "definitely not like a club at school."

"It's more like he got kicked *out* of school for what he wrote," Mitch said.

"Hey, knock it off," Steve said. "I didn't get kicked out!"

"Oh, yeah? Then where'd you disappear to for three weeks?"

"It was a suspension, and you know it."

Nikki glanced over at Keesha, who was starting to look worried. "I . . . don't understand," Nikki said. "Why'd you get suspended for writing a computer game?"

"Because he put it on every terminal in the school," Mitch said with a laugh. "The administration said nobody had ever seen a game with so much gory stuff—the thing was totally blood and guts. You even had a slasher in there somewhere, didn't you, Steve?"

Nikki's fingers tightened on the handle of her fork.

"That's gross," Nikki said flatly. "Are you guys still into that kind of thing?"

Steve sat forward again, carefully balancing the salt shaker on top of the pepper shaker. "Nah, I think we finally grew up. We're more into role-playing games." He looked at Mitch, a half-grin on his face. "In fact, we're working out some of the bugs on the latest one as we speak."

Nikki set her fork across her salad plate. "Working out bugs? What do you mean?"

"We put subjects in different situations and observe how they react." Nikki looked at Mitch closely as he spoke, and couldn't help remembering how much she had always disliked guys with long chins. "Then we enter those reactions into the game."

Steve set the salt and pepper shakers next to each other, then moved them around as if they were walking across the table. "See, in a role-playing game, the players have to actually *become* the character they play, act the way that character would act. In order to write the instructions, we have to observe what real people would do first."

Keesha glanced at Nikki across the table, uneasiness in her dark eyes. "So how did you write the game with the slasher, then?" she asked, laughing nervously. "By cutting people up?"

Steve snorted. "We weren't into role-playing games then. We made stuff up, or watched movies and used that. But what we're doing now is a lot more challenging, much more sophisticated."

She looked at her watch. *Not quite eight o'clock.* She started to think of excuses to leave as Steve went on, his voice growing more and more intense.

"Here's the rules we set for ourselves," he was saying. "We have to put *actual* people in the situations we're creating for the game, and we can only use their *real* responses. So nothing is made up, see? It's totally realistic. That's the genius of what we're doing, the one thing that will make our game different from everyone else's on the market."

Keesha looked down at her dessert plate. "The other guys in this group—are they working on the same game as you?"

"No way," Steve said. "We broke up into pairs, and each pair has to come up with a game. Then we'll judge whose is best. But Mitch and I already know ours is way ahead of the others. We're gonna sell it when we're finished." He leaned over and sucked up the last of his Mountain Dew through the straw.

"So what is this game of yours about?" Keesha asked, her voice cracking a little.

Steve sat back against the booth and held out a hand to indicate that Mitch should go first.

Mitch shifted his position in the booth and hesitated for a few seconds. "Well, it's about, uh, about these two girls who get abducted—"

"*Abducted!*" Keesha broke in. "You mean like in—*kidnapped?*"

One side of Mitch's mouth turned up. "Yeah, but 'abducted' sounds better, don't you think?"

Nikki's eyes narrowed. "And you have to put real people in that situation to see their reactions?" Nikki asked.

"That's right." Steve leaned forward. "*Total realism*—that's what we're after here!"

Nikki pushed her plate away and picked up her purse. "Well, this has been great, just great, to meet you. But I think Keesha and I should—"

Keesha looked up, and Nikki could see she was in total agreement. "Nikki's right—we should probably get going now."

"Get going?" Steve sounded incredulous. "It's only eight o'clock. The night's just starting, babe." He put an arm around Keesha and pulled her close, his mouth against her short, dark hair. "Don't you remember what we said about going down on the beach, later on? We have research to do there."

Mitch reached for Nikki's hand, but she wrenched it away and slid out of the booth. "Come on, Keesha, we really have to get home. You can ride with me—"

Keesha pulled away from Steve with a struggle, and got to her feet beside Nikki.

"Head for the door, Keesha," Nikki said under her breath, "and don't stop walking for anything."

Steve and Mitch were right behind them. "Listen," Steve protested. "You can't go now. We're just getting started here!"

Nikki led the way to the door and pushed it open. She breathed a sigh of relief as she heard the hostess stop Steve and Mitch with a surprisingly shrill, "Have you forgotten something, gentlemen? The *bill*, perhaps?"

As soon as the guys were distracted, Nikki turned to Keesha. "*Run!*" she whispered, and they took off toward the car.

"I *told* you . . . this was . . . dangerous, didn't I?" Nikki said, her voice choppy as she ran. "Now do you . . . see what . . . I meant? Now, hurry up!"

But as they reached the Mazda, Nikki stopped dead and stared.

"What are you waiting for?" Keesha cried, pulling the front door open on the passenger side. "Get in the car!"

"It won't do any good," Nikki said, shaking her head. "Look."

Keesha glanced in the direction Nikki's finger pointed. Both back tires were flat to the rims. "How could *both* tires go at the same time—" Keesha began, but Nikki cut in.

"They couldn't just go flat on their own. Somebody did this. Look at the cuts." She grabbed Keesha's arm. "It doesn't matter. We still have to get out of here. We can run or—"

"Or what?" Mitch's voice sounded behind her. "I think the ladies need some help here, don't you?" he said to Steve, his voice suddenly threatening.

"I think you're absolutely right," Steve said, taking Keesha's arm in a tight grasp. "Our car's right over here—"

Keesha turned and twisted, but Steve had an unbreakable grip on her arm. He propelled her toward a green two-door—something from the 60s, Nikki thought, but in mint condition. Steve opened the driver's side door and pushed Keesha in before him, forcing her to stay close to his side, never letting go of his grip on her arm.

"Ow!" Nikki said as Mitch shoved her in the same direction.

Though he was only a few inches taller than she, it was clear that he was much, much stronger.

Nikki's heart was pounding so hard she could hardly breathe.

On TV, she thought, the victim always figured out some brilliant, last-minute plan to thwart the bad guys. The difference between her and people on TV, she decided, was that terror seemed to sharpen their wits but seemed to freeze hers.

When she found she could not break Mitch's hold on her arms, she moved numbly, trying desperately to think of something she could do or say that would force him to release her.

"You'll never get away with this," she said. "This is kidnapping, and it's a crime—it's got to be. You don't want to spend the rest of your life in prison, do you? And my father's a lawyer—"

Mitch smiled in a way that chilled her. "Keep talking," he said. "I'm keeping track of all these things to input in the game later." He pulled open the passenger side door of the car and pushed the front seat forward, motioning with his head toward the back seat.

Nikki stood as still as if her feet had grown roots into the pavement. She felt absolutely certain that once she got into that car, whatever awful thing Mitch and Steve were planning would come true for sure.

With one hand Mitch motioned in exaggerated fashion toward the seat. He leaned forward from the waist, and Nikki could see the pinpoint pupils of his eyes. "Would you mind getting inside, ma'am?"

Please, God. Please help me! she cried inside.

She managed to stand firm, even against the increasing pressure on her arm. She watched Mitch's eyes comb the parking lot, knowing he was checking to see if he could safely use more force.

God, please, she cried again, and as she did, there came from inside the car a burst of profanity that made even Mitch stop and turn his head.

"What's your problem?" he asked Steve, his voice sharp with annoyance.

"This piece of junk won't even start! Listen to it—it turns over, then nothing. I thought you said you got it fixed!"

Steve turned the key in the ignition several times, pumping the gas. Finally he ordered Mitch to watch Keesha, threw the door open, strode to the front of the car and raised the hood.

"Oh, *this* oughta be good," Mitch muttered. "The guy who knows nothing about cars except how to get speeding tickets, with his head under the hood." He raised his voice. "C'mon, Steve, the ladies are impressed now. You can quit trying to look like Mr. Goodwrench."

Steve looked out from the side of the green hood. "You think you can do better, you go right ahead," he snarled, then let loose with another string of profanity.

Nikki stood by the door, not daring to move, her heart still hammering. She wondered if a car problem counted as an answer to prayer, but had no time to decide as comments between Steve and Mitch turned angrier.

Mitch called to Steve. "What's taking you so long? How hard can it be to figure out? This car was in perfect shape when we drove in here a couple hours ago!"

Steve's head appeared to the side of the hood again, his eyes flashing with anger. He brushed his palms together and walked to Mitch's side. "I'll take care of our company. You go figure it out, since you know everything."

Father, please help us, Nikki prayed once more.

Steve clamped his hand around Nikki's wrist, then yanked her with him as he slid into the front seat beside Keesha. Pain shot through Nikki's right shin as she stumbled into the car, but it was then that she saw the movement out of the corner of her eyes. She swung her head toward the movement, and beyond anything she could have hoped, there was Jeff, walking around the corner of Angelino's toward them. By his side trotted Arleta, hurrying to match her stride to his.

In the glow of the street light, Jeff caught Nikki's glance with his own and gave a barely perceptible shake of his head to warn her. She had almost called out in her excitement at seeing him, but now she closed her mouth and waited silently.

"Having trouble here?" Jeff asked pleasantly once he and Arleta were even with the car. Nikki caught Keesha's eye and shook her head just as Jeff had done. "I don't know too much about cars, but maybe I can help."

Mitch stepped away from the hood and looked Jeff up and down carefully before replying. "Yeah, well, maybe. I've checked everything I can think of and I'm not finding the problem."

"Nice car," Jeff said. "Impala, right? What year?"

"Sixty-four," Mitch said sullenly.

"Restore it yourself?"

"No. I bought it from some guy—" Mitch shook his head impatiently. "We're kind of in a hurry here, all right?"

Nikki was so busy praying she didn't see Arleta leave. She just noticed at some point that the little woman was gone.

Stationed under the hood, Jeff kept up a running commentary on each thing he was checking. Jeff actually had Mitch laughing a couple of times, and Nikki wondered how much he knew about what was really happening here.

Steve's grip on her arm tightened. Stuck in the car between Nikki and Keesha, not daring to reveal that he had one hand restraining each girl, he kept yelling out instructions to Mitch and Jeff.

"Clean the battery terminals," Steve demanded.

"Yeah, we did that first thing," Jeff said.

"Did you clean the air filter?"

"Oh, sure." Jeff's voice was mild and pleasant, and Nikki had the impression he was enjoying this.

Steve brightened up as though he'd just thought of the answer. "Hey! Stick your finger in the carburetor and hold the choke open. The engine must not be getting enough air."

Jeff's voice floated back to them. "Okay, I am. But you pump it so we can look in and make sure the gas is getting through."

Steve pumped it.

"Again!"

Steve hit the gas another time, hard.

"Okay, one more time," Jeff called.

It was then that Steve noticed Arleta's absence. "Hey! Where'd the old lady go?"

Jeff looked out from under the hood. "She went to call some friends of ours who know a lot more about cars than I do."

"*What?*" Steve exploded. "She had no business getting other people involved in this! You go get her."

Jeff held up his hands, smeared with black grease. "Yeah, well, I'm a little busy here. How about you go do that for me? After you hit the gas one more time, that is."

Steve did, and the smell of gasoline seemed to fill the car. He sagged back against the seat and closed his eyes. "That *idiot!* Now the engine's flooded, and it'll *never* start!" He unleashed a torrent of profanity that made Nikki cringe. "Get out from under that hood, you—"

Steve stopped as another vehicle turned into the parking lot, its headlights sweeping the Impala. It was a dark sedan. It stopped, and the man who stepped out had an air of authority. "Could I help, gentlemen?"

Shaking his head, Steve muttered under his breath. "What d'ya got, Good Samaritan types coming out of the walls on this side of the state?" He shouted through the window. "Thanks! I think we can handle this ourselves!"

"You do?" the man said. "Then how about *you* help *me?*" He stretched a long arm through the window toward Steve. "Could I see your license, please?"

In the front of the Impala, Mitch brought his head up so fast he slammed it against the underside of the hood. Nikki heard the thud, then saw him stagger out, his eyes closed tightly and one hand on the painful part. He started to back away, but Jeff grabbed him from behind and held on.

Steve let go of the girls' arms, then struggled to make his way out of the front seat. Keesha did a half turn, covering the door with her body. Steve pushed and pulled at her, but couldn't get enough leverage to budge her. Nikki grabbed the back of his shirt and hung on with all her might.

The stranger pulled a police badge from an inside pocket and dangled it in front of Steve's face. Next came a gun, leveled at Steve. Suddenly, all struggling ceased; even though Nikki knew this meant rescue, she felt a thrill of terror at the sight of the gun barrel pointing in her direction.

Nikki sagged against the seat. She looked forward to getting out of the car, but wasn't sure she'd be able to walk when she did. Her legs were shaking.

Almost immediately, the noise of other cars sounded from the front of Angelino's. Two police cruisers pulled into the parking lot; in less than a minute uniformed men clamped handcuffs on Steve and Mitch, reciting the boys' rights in singsong tones.

Meanwhile, Arleta reappeared from the direction of the restaurant. She marched to the side of the man who had appeared in the dark sedan, hands on her hips.

"ARNOLD," she demanded, her voice a mixture of pride and exasperation, "WHAT TOOK YOU SO LONG?"

❦ *Sixteen* ❧

BEFORE NIKKI COULD TAKE IN all that was happening, Mitch and Steve were gone, safely locked inside the back seat of a police cruiser.

She managed to get out of the car, then stood there watching until her knees began to buckle. She felt Jeff's arms go around her gently, helping her back onto the Impala seat.

You did it, God, she kept thinking numbly. *You did it.*

Within a few minutes, half the people she knew seemed to have crowded into the parking lot. Her grandparents and her mother were there. The Allens arrived. Everyone was asking questions at once.

Most surprising of all, Keesha's mother was with them.

If she hadn't been so relieved to see them, Nikki thought, she would have been embarrassed at having the entire family turn out in force to rescue them. As it was, she couldn't seem to stop the tears that trickled down her cheeks.

Keesha, leaning against the hood and supported by her mother, was crying, too. The twins stood off to one side, worried looks on their faces.

One of the police officers, who'd been sitting in the front of his car with his door open, talking on the radio, now returned to the Impala. "We'll need to get these girls to the hospital," he said, apparently unsure of who to address. "Have them checked over and make sure they're all right."

Grandpa spoke up. "We'll be right there, sir. As soon as they have a few minutes to catch their breath."

The officer nodded, smiling. "We'll need to fill out a report, too, but we'll try not to ask too many questions."

But Nikki had some questions of her own. As soon as she felt steady enough, she stood to her feet and faced Jeff. "How did you know where we were?"

Jeff waved a hand at the group standing there. "Everybody kind of worked together. Otherwise, we would have never figured out what was going on. The twins finally gave us the missing piece."

Nikki blinked in surprise. "The twins? How—"

Grandpa held up both hands. "Could we save the questions until we're done at the hospital? The police are waiting. Then we can all meet at home and talk this thing out."

It was late by the time they gathered at the house. Nikki found it hard to believe that only a week had passed since her birthday party when, except for Keesha's mother, they'd all been right here together.

Nikki dropped onto the hassock, the only seat left. "Could you just start at the beginning, please, and tell me how you knew where we were?"

"Just a little bit after you left," Jeff began, "Keesha's mom called your grandma. She was really upset because—"

"Because I found that letter of yours, the one off the computer!" Keesha's mother broke in. She turned to her daughter, who squirmed on the couch beside her.

"What were you doing reading my *mail?*" Keesha demanded, then withered under her mother's stare.

"Well, apparently somebody *needed* to be reading your mail, young lady," her mom declared. "I did some of Serena's laundry and was putting it away in your room, trying to help you a little, and the letter was sitting right there in full view."

"She got a bit nervous when she read it," Gram put in.

"Nervous is putting it *mildly*—very, very *mildly*," Mrs. Riley said.

"The way any mother would, I'm sure," Gram continued. "The letter just said you were meeting somebody named Steve for dinner, and that he had to drive three hours from Detroit and that you were trying to get Nikki to come with you."

"But it didn't say where you were meeting!" Mrs. Riley cried. "I just had the first page. So I called over here, figuring Carole and Roger would know what was going on. I just had that feeling you were in trouble."

"But of course, we didn't have a clue where you'd gone," Gram added.

"The twins heard all this," Jeff said, "and Abby finally came to me and told me what they'd been doing with the e-mail."

"And we will be dealing with this issue later, you understand," Dr. Allen said, looking at Abby and Adam sternly. "For right now, I think an apology to Nikki is in order."

Abby hung her head. "We're sorry, Nikki," she mumbled. "We weren't trying to cause trouble for you."

"Abby just thought it'd be funny, you know?" Adam said. "And maybe even kind of romantic, 'cause when we read that guy's letter to you, it sounded like he really liked you . . ." Adam's voice dwindled away as everyone's eyes fixed on him. "Okay, so it was stupid. And wrong. I'm sorry, too. But we were the ones who told everybody where you were, Nikki!"

"That's true, they did," Jeff said. "We were all trying to figure out where you were, and how we were supposed to find you in case something was wrong. That's when Abby said she thought she might know where you were.

"As soon as she told me, I jumped in the Bronco and got to Angelino's as fast as I could. I told Abby to tell the others, and I knew they'd get help. Arleta must have followed me eventually."

Arleta nodded. "THAT'S RIGHT," she said. "JUST AFTER I CALLED ARNOLD."

"I parked on the street," Jeff continued, "on the other side of the trees, and had just turned off the Bronco when I saw that guy come out of the restaurant to the parking lot. I ducked down, and he must've thought the truck was empty. Next thing I knew, he was slashing the tires on the Mazda. I wanted to take him out right then and there, but I knew I'd better wait and call the police. Never got the chance, though, because you all came out too soon."

Nikki gave a huge sigh. "You won't believe how God answered my prayer. Mitch and Steve were forcing us into the car, and I just started praying God would help us. And just like that—" she snapped her fingers "—their car wouldn't start! They said it'd been running great up till then."

She snapped her fingers again for emphasis. "Just like that! Can you believe it?"

Jeff and Arleta looked at each other and burst out laughing.

"What?" Nikki asked. "What's so funny? You don't believe God answers prayer now?"

Jeff said, "Sure I do, Nikki, you know that." Then he started laughing again.

Nikki stared at him, looking as angry as she could.

Jeff held up both hands. "Don't get mad, Nik! I'm not laughing at you. I *do* believe God answers our prayers, but sometimes He does it through other people, you know?" He turned to Arleta. "You better show her, Arleta, or I'm about to get in big trouble."

Arleta reached into her pocket, pulled out a thin piece of wire, and held it up for inspection.

Nikki frowned. "Well, that's a big help. Now tell me what it is."

"It's the coil wire," Jeff explained. "From Steve's Impala."

"You took the coil wire off his distributor?" Dr. Allen demanded.

Jeff shrugged, trying to look innocent. "Hey, Arleta told me to do it. And you taught me to always listen to my elders, right?"

"WE HAD TO DO SOMETHING TO GIVE THE POLICE TIME TO GET THERE AND RESCUE NIKKI AND KEESHA," Arleta defended him. "AND DON'T WORRY, IT DOESN'T DO ANY PERMANENT DAMAGE. WE'LL GIVE IT BACK."

Jeff started laughing again, trying to tell his side of the story. "I knew which one was their car, because after that guy slashed your tires, he went over and tossed something into the Impala—probably the knife he used. When Arleta drove up and I told her we needed to stop them, she said it was easy—just take the coil wire off the distributor. And the rest, as they say, is history."

"But I don't understand something, Arleta," Nikki said. "Why did you go to the restaurant?"

Arleta looked down for a moment. When she raised her head, Nikki saw she was near tears. "I KNOW THAT SOMETIMES I'M JUST AN INTERFERING OLD WOMAN. BUT I'VE BEEN PRAYING FOR YOU SINCE YOU WERE BORN, NIKKI SHERIDAN, AND I WAS PRAYING FOR YOU TONIGHT. SO WHEN I HEARD WHAT WAS GOING ON, I JUST GOT IN THE CAR AND DROVE AS FAST AS I COULD TO WHERE YOU WERE. I CALLED ARNOLD, BUT I JUST HAD THIS SENSE THAT THERE WAS SOMETHING FOR ME TO DO, TOO."

She fumbled in her pocket for a tissue, and blew her nose loudly. "SOMETIMES WHEN YOU PRAY YOU HAVE TO WAIT FOR AN ANSWER. BUT OTHER TIMES YOU GET TO *BE* THE ANSWER, YOU KNOW?"

Keesha shook her head in amazement. "But how did you know to disconnect the wire from the . . . the whatever it was? I mean, how'd you ever come up with an idea like that?"

Arleta looked at her as though the answer was obvious. "ARE YOU TELLING ME YOU'VE NEVER WATCHED *THE SOUND OF MUSIC?*"

"Um . . . no, I guess I haven't," Keesha said.

"WELL, COME BY THE LIBRARY AND CHECK IT OUT," Arleta said. "THAT'S WHAT THEY DID IN THE MOVIE."

By the time they got the entire story figured out, then spent another half hour talking about Steve and Mitch and what a close call it had been for Nikki and Keesha, it was long after midnight.

More than anything, Nikki had longed for a moment to talk to Jeff alone, to thank him for what he'd done. But there was no way to be alone with the house so full of people. Finally, when they'd all cleared out and her grandparents and mother had gone upstairs to bed, Nikki found herself alone in the kitchen.

Surprised to find herself hungry, she stuck a bagel in the toaster and checked the refrigerator for cream cheese. She was pulling it out from behind the milk when she heard a quick, quiet knock at the kitchen door and turned to see Jeff standing there.

"Are they all gone?" he asked with a grin, but his eyes were serious.

"Yeah, everybody went home, finally." The toaster popped, and she took the bagel out and put it on the waiting plate.

Jeff looked down at her, studying her face. "And what about you? Are you going to be all right?"

"You mean about tonight?"

He nodded.

Nikki thought back over the evening. "I think so, Jeff. I—there's just so many things to process. Like what the police told us at the hospital, about guys like Steve and Mitch and how they hurt people." Arnold, Arleta's son, had been especially blunt in describing some of the cases he'd seen in his last few years on the police force. When he finished, he'd snapped his notebook shut and stood up, looming over them. His final words still rang in her ears. *"I want to make sure you understand how unwise it was for you to meet those guys in person, especially without an adult around. Let's just say you two were very, very lucky."*

Jeff took the plate out of her hands, spread cream cheese on her bagel, then held it back toward her. "You might want to eat this while it's still warm, Nik."

Nikki looked down at the plate and smiled. "Thanks, Jeff. Guess I got sidetracked there for a minute." She held out half the bagel toward him. "Want some?"

"Well, sure, if you're offering—"

Nikki took a bite of her half and chewed thoughtfully. There were so many things she wanted to say to Jeff, but she didn't have any idea how to begin.

But he spoke first. "Nikki? I just wanted to say how . . . how glad I am. That nothing worse happened tonight. That you didn't get hurt."

She looked up into those dark blue eyes and saw something there that made her set her plate down on the counter. "You are?"

"Oh, yeah. I really am." He put his arms around her gently and pulled her close.

"Nikki, listen. I know what you said last year, about just wanting us to be friends. And I've tried, I really have."

He paused. "But it's not working."

Nikki stepped back to see his face and tried to make sense of his words. "Wait a minute. What about Shannon? When I tried to talk to you tonight, it was more important to you to take her phone call—"

Jeff started shaking his head back and forth as soon as she said "Shannon," and by the time she brought up the phone call, he could stand it no longer. "Nikki! You never gave me a chance to explain. I thought when I went off to college that it was time to find someone else. It was obvious to me that you really meant what you said about us being friends. So when Shannon started hanging around, I tried, Nik. I told myself, 'She's pretty, she's smart—' "

"And has perfect teeth," Nikki murmured under her breath, but Jeff didn't notice.

"But then last week, at the birthday party, you started acting like you really cared about me again. That threw me. I realized that all the old feelings for you were still there. Then I was really in a mess. I didn't know what to do. Finally I left a message for Shannon at school, trying to explain, and that's what she was calling me about this afternoon. She was really upset, and I needed to say something to her. But you just took off, so how could I explain?" he finished in exasperation, his arms spread wide in question.

Nikki frowned. "I thought you were looking down on me."

"*What?*"

"That morning on the dune, you know, when I told you about my dad leaving us? You hardly said anything, and I thought it was because my family is so . . . so *not* like yours."

Jeff ran his open hand through his hair, pushing it back off his forehead. "No, Nik, that wasn't it at all. I was thinking how stupid it was that I didn't have a clue what to say. Seems like a Christian ought to know what to say at a time like that, but I didn't."

Nikki set her plate on the counter and wadded up her napkin

on top of it. "And here all the time, I thought you were comparing me to Shannon."

His blue eyes brightened a little. "I was, Nikki. I was."

She gave a short laugh. "Well, given all of Shannon's rather obvious charms, I'd be curious to hear what's wrong with her—"

Jeff put one finger against her lips to still them. "Wrong with her? There's just one thing wrong with Shannon, Nikki. She's not you—she's not *you.*"

❧ *Epilogue* ❧

Sun, 12 Sept, 18:35:04
Dear Jeff,

I've pretty much sworn off e-mail. But since it's you, I guess it's okay! Anyway, since you had to leave after church this morning, I need to tell you some pretty incredible news.

You already know that Mom didn't go back to Ohio yesterday morning. I think she may have been more shook up about what happened Friday night than Keesha and I were. I had asked her to come to Arleta's tea and hear me talk, but she'd been giving me one excuse after another, so I really didn't expect her to be there. But she was!

In a way, seeing her there was great. In another way, it made me even more nervous. I mean, giving any kind of speech is hard enough, let alone doing it in front of your own mother.

Remember how stressed out I was yesterday because I still couldn't come up with something to say? No matter how I tried, I couldn't even find time to work on it, what with everything that's gone on this past week. But I think now that I wasn't supposed to go with a canned speech. I think God wanted me to just talk about what was important to me.

When I got up there in front of those people (67 in all, including

165

Hollis and Noel and their friends, who sat right in the front row), all I could do was tell them what happened to me this past year. I was so nervous beforehand that I didn't think I'd be able to talk, but Arleta kept whispering (if you can imagine that!) in my ear beforehand that if I asked the Lord to, He would use what I said.

I didn't think what I said was much, but about halfway through, I finally got the nerve to look up. My mother was sitting right there, crying. Right in front of everyone, Jeff. And when the tea was over, she asked me to go for a drive with her and we talked for a couple of hours.

She told me all about how she was so disappointed when she was young and found out Grandpa wasn't her real father, and how she got angry at God and just shut the door on Him for good. And then she said she could see now how things could have been if she hadn't turned her back on Him, and she wanted to get everything straightened out. And then we prayed together. Can you *believe* this?

And to top it all off, Hollis and Noel—who made me really nervous during the speech—came up to me after the tea and asked me to have lunch with them next week so we could talk. I don't know where that one will end up, but I'll let you know.

About my parents—well, Mom obviously doesn't want to talk about it much, so I'll just wait for her to bring it up. But I can tell you one thing. God's been answering my prayers—at least some of them—right away. I can see now that He doesn't answer all my prayers on *my* schedule, but Grandpa keeps telling me that waiting is the hardest thing to deal with when it comes to prayer, so I'm going to keep praying. And waiting.

Sometimes I don't think we're supposed to know what's going to happen. I think we're supposed to ask what God wants, pray that it will happen, and then just stand still and wait.

It's getting late, so I'd better close. Are you sure you're going to have time to write every day? Let me know, and please keep praying for my parents. If God can change my mother this way, He can change *any*one!

Talk to you tomorrow,
Nikki

The NIKKI SHERIDAN SERIES
by Shirley Brinkerhoff

Choice Summer
Mysterious Love
Narrow Walk
Balancing Act
Tangled Web